DRAKE

INTERGALACTIC DATING AGENCY

DRAGON BRIDES
BOOK 6

KATE RUDOLPH

ABOUT THE BOOK

Danger stalks a downed ship in an alien jungle…

When Drake receive a distress call from a nearby planet he has to respond. People need help, and it allows him to focus on something other than the devastating news delivered by the Royal Matchmaker. But he can't believes what he finds when he and his crew discover the survivors.

She's on the adventure of a lifetime…

Claudia might have been born a simple Earth girl, but she's spent the last few years traversing the discovery and seeing things people back home would never believe. But she doesn't want to end up as monster chow on an alien planet. When Drake arrives, she lets herself believe they just might escape.

But an invisible monster is hunting them. How can

the fight a monster they can't see? She needs to focus on survival, but she can't take her eyes off the way-too-hot dragon who's stealing all her attention.

CHAPTER
ONE

AS THE YOUNGEST of his three brothers, Drake had never expected to be named his mother's heir. Cipher had always seemed like the perfect dragon, and until two days ago, there had been no question about who would lead the family when it was time.

But now…

Drake wasn't a born leader. He didn't want the responsibility. But the condition didn't rankle him, not like it did for his brothers. Cipher and Storm were ready to start some kind of rebellion rather than accede to their mother's wish and find suitable brides.

Drake had been looking for a bride of his own forever. Or at least it felt that way.

He'd never visited the Royal Matchmaker, though. There was something about it that felt a little like cheating. Rumor had it the matchmaker was some sort of psychic and was never wrong. Not only had it felt like cheating, there was a little fear there.

What if the bride she pointed him to was someone else who would find him… lacking? His last lady love had left him for a dragon who was a keen explorer and could dazzle a room with stories of his daring feats and near death dramas.

Drake had never ridden on top of a spaceship while narrowly escaping pirates and shooting fire to cover the escape of a bunch of people rescued from slavers' clutches. But the women he was drawn to, the women he flirted with and wined and dined, the ones he hoped would accept his heart and a place in his life always expected it of him.

And he never lived up to it.

He almost turned on his heel and fled when he started down the road to the Royal Matchmaker's shop. His mother had set up a meeting for him and each of his brothers before she left on a year-long diplomatic mission, but it didn't mean that he had to find his bride through her. He had a year to find someone suitable.

That was plenty of time.

Wasn't it?

He may have not been a mighty adventurer, but he was a trained soldier and a dragon lord. He could take a single meeting. If he didn't like what the matchmaker said, he didn't have to act on it. Still, when he came to the door, he hesitated. It was only when someone bumped into him that he realized he was blocking the sidewalk.

He walked in.

It wasn't what he expected.

Of course, Drake had never been in any matchmaker's shop before. He wasn't exactly sure how the process was supposed to work. But this place looked a bit like a sitting room he would expect in his mother's estate.

There was a sofa opposite two comfortable chairs with a table in the middle. On the other side of the room there was a small round table flanked by two chairs on spindly legs. Along one wall was a sideboard with small sandwiches, cakes, and a machine that could make various beverages at the press of a button.

He hadn't known there'd be cake.

But there wasn't any matchmaker.

A curtain separated the front of the shop from the back, and he assumed she was back there. He hadn't heard a bell or anything when he came in, so she might not yet realize he was there. He wondered if he should go find her, but hesitated. Instead, he walked slowly around the room, taking his time to check out the cakes and then test the softness of the cushions on the couch.

He was fiddling with the golden tassels fringing a pillow when she walked out. She was a bit older than him, with light brown skin, a purple scarf covering her hair, and bright blue eyes that seemed to buzz with electricity.

"May I help you, sir?" she asked, her voice a bit lower than he expected. Sultry.

Drake shot to his feet and reflexively gave a short, respectful bow. "I have an appointment, ma'am." Wouldn't a psychic know that?

Her eyes sparkled as if she knew the question he hadn't asked. "I see. My name is Shade and I'm the Royal Matchmaker. May I have yours?"

"Lord Drake." He forced himself not to look out the front window to see who was passing by on the street. Word would soon spread that he and his brothers were on the hunt for brides, and he would like to hold off those rumors for as long as he could.

Shade smiled and approached him, holding out a hand. He clasped hers when she got close enough and let go after a faint squeeze. "Would you care for tea or some food?" she asked. "There's plenty."

He wondered if it was some sort of test, if she was checking to see what sort of man he was. Did it matter if he chose a sandwich rather than a cake? Did tea mean something different than coffee? Or were they just snacks?

He didn't let himself overthink it, grabbing a small cake that made his mouth water and preparing a coffee just as he liked it. Shade served herself an identical cake and a floral smelling tea.

They sat back down and sipped their drinks while eating their snacks. Shade watched him the entire time. But Drake had spent a lifetime being observed every moment he was out in public and didn't let it bother him.

He finished his cake. "Delicious."

"Thank you. One of the local bakeries prepares the dishes. This is a bit more than usual. They've been testing products for an upcoming event they're catering." She took a sip of tea and then leaned back in her chair. "So, Lord Drake, you've come to find a bride."

They were starting. Right. Drake sat up straighter and took a final sip of his coffee before setting it down. "I am, yes." A part of him was tempted to launch into a recounting of his entire failed history of finding a proper bride, but he held his tongue. If this Shade was psychic, she could discern that herself.

"Would you hold out your hand for me?" she asked.

"Is this... there are rumors you're psychic." He didn't know what she could see if she looked at his palm, and he wasn't sure he wanted her looking deep into his soul.

But what if she saw something important? What if she saw his mate?

Drake quashed the thought. Mates were a rare gift, and though he'd been looking for a bride for years, he'd never thought he'd really find his mate.

"There are always rumors," Shade replied, then she motioned for him to give her his hand.

He held it out, palm up.

Shade stared at it from a meter away for a few moments before leaning in. She didn't touch him, but she did angle her body to look at his hand from any way she could manage. When she instructed, he flipped it over and she looked again.

"Hmmm." She leaned back. "Interesting."

Drake let his hand drop and tried not to shiver. He didn't love the way Shade was looking at him. She remained silent for several moments.

He couldn't take it any longer. "What?"

She thought for another moment before answering. "If you seek your mate now, you will lose her forever."

"What's that supposed to mean?" Only long ingrained manners kept him from jumping out of his chair and demanding more. His tone was harsher than it should have been.

"I can find you a suitable bride, my lord. Or you can think on what I've said. If you'd like to move forward, contact me next week and we'll set up a second appointment." She stood.

He followed. There were questions he needed answered. What kind of pronouncement was that? What kind of meeting was *this*? Had he even been with her for a quarter hour? He needed to find a bride, so why was she sending him away?

And how could he find his mate if he couldn't look for her?

"My job is as much research as it is intuition, my lord. Please allow me the time I'll need to help you. If you call me." She ushered him to the door so cleverly that he was practically outside before he realized he was moving.

Drake didn't fight it. What was the point?

One thing was certain. He'd find his bride on his own before subjecting himself to more of that nonsense.

CHAPTER
TWO

CLAUDIA BUTLER WAS on a freaking spaceship. With aliens. Aliens were real! And she was in space! Even after three years, the wonder still hit her at times. Growing up in small town Ohio, her dreams had been to one day make it to a big city like Pittsburgh, or maybe Chicago.

Leaving the planet never to return? That hadn't been in the cards until a crazy rich guy with *ideas* came calling. Sometimes it hurt to know that she had no return ticket home, that her family was back there with no idea if the experimental wormhole journey had worked. But she'd earned them huge piles of money, and they would never know a moment of discomfort.

And she got to explore space and learn the secrets of the universe.

Though right now, that exploration felt a little bit like living in the bowels of some cargo ship traversing a vast ocean. She was the only passenger on this small mercenary ship. They were headed across the galaxy and had been willing to let her book passage to a smaller planet that was looking for human workers.

That was another trip. Apparently, Claudia was far from the only human living off of Earth.

She would have been kicking her heels for weeks at a space station if she waited to find a passenger ship headed that way. But plenty of merc crews took passengers between jobs, and often the quarters were nearly as good—or better!—than third class on a passenger ship. Sure, Claudia had to pitch in with a bit of the cleaning and cooking, but that was easy enough.

And the crew wasn't too bad.

Usually.

Right now, she could do with a bit of space. But Ruzo had her cornered. He was seven and a half feet tall, and had huge horns growing out of his head, tusks coming out of his jaw, and bluish green skin. He'd been flirting with her since she'd boarded and didn't take the hint from her deflections that she wasn't interested.

He wasn't the freakiest alien she'd ever seen, not

by far. But the horns and the tusks threw her off her step.

"Come on," he was saying, "let's go play a round of Triplex. Friendly wagers only." He stood close enough to touch, but she didn't think he meant to be threatening.

He was just so *big* that her heart rate couldn't help but kick up when she realized just how much space he dominated.

"I don't know how to play that," she said. She'd learned several popular games during her journeys over the last three years, but Triplex didn't sound familiar.

Ruzo's face brightened and he smiled, flashing the serrated teeth in his mouth. "I can teach you!"

He sounded so excited that Claudia forced herself not to react to the teeth. She didn't want to be rude, didn't want him thinking that she was some sort of anti-alien person or whatever. She was an alien too.

But those teeth were really freaking sharp. She'd seen sharks that looked less toothy.

The lights overhead flickered, and a small squeak escaped her. Ruzo clamped a large hand on her shoulder and she stiffened. But he didn't notice. Or, perhaps, he thought it was because of the lights and not him. "Happens sometimes," he explained, "especially when the engines have to shift. Nothing to worry—"

The lights went out completely, and the ship jolted hard enough to send them crashing into the wall behind them. She could feel the heat of Ruzo's arms as he braced them on the wall, holding himself up to keep from crushing her.

"Alright, Claud?" he asked. He wasn't touching her this time.

Claudia could feel the warm impression of him in the air in front of her, and she knew where he was by the sound of his voice. But it was pitch black in the hallway. She counted to five in her head, hoping the lights would come back on when she opened her eyes.

Then she realized she'd never closed them.

She bit her lip to keep from whimpering. Claudia wouldn't call herself a coward, but she really didn't like the dark.

The playful flirting Ruzo had been shooting her way was gone when he next spoke, and he was all business and self-assurance. "Grab onto my belt," he told her. "I'm going to guide you to the nearest seat and get you strapped in. Then I'll check what's up. You're safe."

Any of the apprehension at his flirting melted away with his confidence, and Claudia willingly followed him to the promised seat. It wasn't far. He guided her down and had her strapped in, though even he had a bit of an issue getting the harness properly over her head when neither of them could see.

"Captain will get this sorted," he promised. "Stay here until I come and get you or you hear the all clear."

Then he was gone.

Claudia squeezed her eyes shut so hard the muscles in her face started to cramp. But she needed that assurance that her eyes were closed. If they were closed, that meant she controlled the darkness. Then she used one of the breathing exercises she'd been taught during the year of training she'd endured before the mission through the wormhole.

Three short breaths in, one long breath out. One long breath in, three short out. One long in, one long out. Repeat.

It was something to focus on rather than the way all the sounds around her were amplified. Had Ruzo made it to the captain? Were the others okay? What was the situation with the life support?

She made herself breathe again. And again. And again.

She had just started to calm down and believe that whatever was wrong would be fixed soon when the ship jolted again. Something crashed to the floor. Then her ears popped and her limbs started to float of their own volition.

The gravity drive had failed.

That was her last full thought before the ship gave a final jolt and whiteness flashed behind Claudia's eyes.

She didn't have a final thought as she lost consciousness and the ship fell out of space.

SHADE'S WORDS echoed around Drake's head for the next two days, and he couldn't stop the restless, angry energy they summoned up within him. He'd learned to control his smoke at a young age, but he'd been surrounded by a cloud of the stuff every moment he let his thoughts wander. Stars above, if this kept up, his control would be worse than Storm's.

Flying didn't help either. He did it for hours, eating up the sky and pushing himself until his wings threatened to give out.

What was so wrong with him that he couldn't have a mate? He was an honorable dragon. He wanted a woman to bring into his home and spoil senseless. He knew he'd be a good mate.

And Shade said he wouldn't have a chance.

What did she know?

Rumors might abound that she was some sort of psychic, but he didn't believe in nonsense. All she'd done was stare at his hand for a minute and make some sort of pronouncement. It didn't mean anything. She could easily guess he wouldn't find his mate. Mates were relatively rare, so most people didn't. She could have been bluffing.

Deep in his soul, he didn't believe it. And he was a bit terrified to go off in search of his mythical mate just in case Shade was right.

Maybe this was some kind of cruel game. She'd teased him with the taunt that he wouldn't find his mate so he would be forced to crawl back to her and seek her help to find a suitable partner. Or perhaps his mother had put her up to it, trying to match him with a dragoness of her choosing rather than whatever mate was out there.

No. Even in his darkest moments, Drake didn't think that. Not because his mother cared so much for his future happiness, but because if she was going to meddle so closely in the affairs of one of her sons, it would be Cipher. Drake was the spare's spare. His mother normally only cared that he didn't actively embarrass the family. If she wanted him to do something, she—or more likely, one of her assistants—would tell him what she wished.

Drake wasn't fit for company, but he'd forced

himself off of his estate and into a large park on the edge of a nearby village. Walking in his land bound skin made him feel strangely heavy, even though this form was so much smaller than his dragon form. But if flying wouldn't help, perhaps walking would.

He could look for her.

The thought came at him sideways. It had been swirling around for a while, but now it appeared fully formed. He knew his mate wasn't one of the proper dragon ladies of the court. He'd met all of them many times, and he'd even had relationships with a few of them. No, none of them were for him. But Shade had implied his mate was out there somewhere.

And he could go looking for her.

Was she a peasant? Some poor dragoness working as a servant in a noble house? A teacher in one of their schools? Was she on Vemion at all? Perhaps she lived in one of the far off colonies.

Was she even a dragon?

The thought brought him up short. If his mate wasn't a dragon, then she could be anywhere in the galaxy. Finding her would be impossible.

But Drake could be dedicated to a cause when he wanted something bad enough.

"Drake! There you are!" His friend Sentinel's voice cut through his thoughts.

Drake paused to let him catch up. He and Sentinel

had known each other since their school days, but hadn't seen each other in some time. Sentinel had some sort of business that often took him off planet. "It's good to see you," he said, because manners mattered even when he was in a terrible mood.

"I'm glad I found you. I heard in the tavern you've been stalking the skies. My ship picked up a distress call on a nearby planet. My crew has mostly scattered on the winds for their leave, and I can't call them back in time. I'm putting together a rescue crew, and I remember how good you are in a tough spot. Will you help? We leave as soon as I fill out the roster, should just be a couple more hours." He had the serious look he'd worn during training missions, the one that let Drake know he wouldn't be winning whatever competition their instructors cooked up for them.

But this was no training mission. "Of course, I'm in. Where shall I meet you?"

Sentinel clapped him on the shoulder and gave him the directions. They didn't talk for long; Sentinel had to find more dragons to round out the crew.

Drake put thoughts of his mate aside for the moment. He could find her later. The rescue mission had to come first.

———

Drake was the only member of the rescue crew who wasn't a normal part of Sentinel's crew. The captain had been able to summon back two of his people, Fluke and Vise, and they'd shipped out before nightfall.

"How long ago did you pick up the signal?" Drake asked as they flew into orbit. It was daytime on this planet, and the flight had only taken a few hours. This planet was in the same system as Vemion, though not inhabited by anyone but the native flora and fauna. Something had prevented dragons from trying to set up outposts, and the planet was listed in their nav system as hostile to foreign life, though the air composition, gravity, and other indicators all showed that dragons could flourish there.

"Nearly ten hours ago now." Sentinel was in the navigator seat while Vise flew the ship. Fluke was cleaning his knives and strapping them to his belt. Most dragons were content to use their warrior forms or their flame as weapons with no need for anything else. Fluke, apparently, liked a bit of backup.

"Not your fault, cap." Vise gave him a tight nod, then turned her attention back to the view-screen in front of her. "I'm seeing a lot of jungle down there. And there's definitely a crash site. Heat signature suggests there's an engine burning through its fuel.

Seems steady, but you know how those can go nova on a whim."

"Any signs of survivors?" Sentinel asked.

"The engine's too hot to get a reading."

Sentinel grunted out an acknowledgement. "I don't want us landing too close to the ship in case it goes nova." The captain turned to Drake and Fluke. "I want the two of you to fly down there while we hover and check out the site. Quickly. If there are signs of life, we'll find a place to park."

"Engaging hover mode," Vise confirmed, flicking a few switches on her controls.

Drake and Fluke headed towards the ship's loading bay.

"You remember how to shift in midair?" Fluke asked, a hint of challenge in his voice. His accent indicated that he wasn't highborn, and the scars on his hands and face showed he was a fighter.

Drake wasn't about to rise to the challenge. They were here to rescue people. If Fluke needed to show off, Drake would let him. "I think I've got it."

Fluke slammed his hand down on the door release and an alarm sounded, warning them. A moment later, the air whipped around them and the roar of the engines threatened to deafen him. As soon as he had the room, Fluke sprinted and jumped, shifting forms seamlessly once he'd cleared the ship. Drake followed right after, doing the same and careful to stay out of Fluke's flight path.

They glided down to the ground and both shifted to human before their dragon forms could do any damage.

Around them, the forest threatened to swallow them up, and Drake shifted to his warrior form to use his claws to break through stubborn vines. Fluke used his knives.

The debris field started with twists of smoking metal and piles of ash. Seeing that, Drake wondered how anyone could survive. But as they got deeper into the field, they could see that the ship was mostly intact. Whatever had happened, the pilot had managed to crash as safely as was possible.

No bodies outside.

"I'll check inside," Fluke declared. "Cover me."

Drake didn't argue. He didn't know if there were multiple entrances to the ship, but he didn't explore, instead waiting for Fluke to finish his search. Hopefully the onboard computer was still functioning and could scan for life. Otherwise, it could take hours to search a ship that big.

The back of Drake's neck itched, and he surveyed the forest around him. It felt like someone was watching him. But places like this always felt like that. This planet's life forms were mostly insects, birds, and rodents. There was nothing big enough out there that could truly do him harm unless he ate a poisonous frog or something like that.

But the feeling of surveillance didn't go away.

Fluke came out before Drake could think about exploring the edge of the jungle. "Nothing," he said. "Checked the onboard computer. No life forms. No bodies. We're looking for three crew and one passenger."

Drake took another look at the wreckage. "This is a lot of ship for three crew."

"There was a roster. The rest are listed as on a job. I copied as much of the data as I could." He held up a small storage device before slipping it into a pouch on his belt. "Come on, we need to finish our check before reporting back."

They split up to walk the circumference of the ship, but it wasn't long before Drake was calling for Fluke as loud as he could. The other dragon came running.

Claw marks raked down the hull of the ship, and a splash of something that looked an awful lot like blood pooled on the ground below. Drake knelt down and touched it. "It's been a bit since this was spilled."

"But someone was definitely alive." Fluke looked out into the jungle. "And I don't think they're alone."

CLAUDIA BARFED. Again.

This time, Krax and Seris didn't even notice as the three of them tried to fight their way through the jungle as if they had any idea where they were going. If it weren't for them, Claudia would still be frozen in terror outside the ship, staring at the spot where Ruzo had been standing when some invisible thing had attacked him and snatched him away as if he weighed nothing.

"Keep up, girl, we're not slowing down." Krax grunted it over his shoulder as if Claudia wasn't less than five feet behind them.

This wasn't the first time she'd regretted signing up to explore space, but it was definitely the worst. It was one thing to know you might die in the middle of a mission, but she'd survived that. And over the last few years, she'd begun to think she might be able to carve a life for herself somewhere in the stars.

It wasn't supposed to end getting hunted by an invisible monster in a space jungle!

She washed out her mouth with a few swigs of water from her canteen and spat it out. Then she took an actual drink of water before securing the canteen back where it belonged on her pack. She knew Krax and Seris had heavier packs, but that didn't make her shoulders burn any less from the strain.

She focused on that. Pain meant she wasn't thinking about Ruzo's blood spraying like that.

And she was thinking about it again.

Seris dropped back to walk beside Claudia. She rested a comforting blue hand on Claudia's shoulder and offered her a smile that would have been a bit more reassuring if her mouth wasn't full of fangs. Then again, if there was a monster out there, Claudia was probably safer if she had monsters protecting her. "We've got to find a safe place to make camp," Seris told her gently. "I know this can't be pleasant, but we'll make it through this. We were able to broadcast a distress signal before we crashed, and we're not too far from populated planets. There's a good chance someone will find us."

"Before whatever got Ruzo finds us?" She was

going to be seeing that blood spray in her nightmares for the rest of her life.

She'd never hoped nightmares would last for longer than the next day.

A strange look crossed Seris' face before it was wiped away and she was all business again. "We can't dwell on that. We have to save ourselves first." She hurried on to catch back up with Krax.

One foot in front of the other. That was all Claudia had to do. No wasting time thinking about the crash or Ruzo. Just footsteps.

The jungle that pressed in on her reminded her of a vacation her family had taken to Guatemala before the money ran out and their dreams became a lot smaller. She wondered if this planet had birds as amazing as she'd seen on that vacation, the brightly beaked toucans and quetzals with magnificent tails.

She couldn't see any animals, but the jungle seemed to teem with life. The vines and branches cracked, leaves rustled, and there were chirps and calls from high up in the canopy.

Whatever had taken Ruzo hadn't killed everything on the planet.

Damn it! Had she even made it ten steps without circling back to that?

Krax and Seris really were speeding ahead of her now, and Claudia jogged to catch up. She didn't feel like she was being followed, but how would she know? She needed to get close to the aliens with giant fangs and even gianter blasters. She didn't even have a knife, and she realized now that maybe that was an issue.

"Hey!" she forced herself to call to the mercenaries in front of her. She didn't do it quietly, either. Maybe if there were big animals, she might scare them away. Or something.

Krax cast a glance over his shoulder. "You decided to catch up?"

"I think I should be carrying a blaster." Krax had four small ones in holsters all over his body in addition to the large, rifle-like weapon he carried.

He pursed his lips and scrunched his forehead, giving her an intense look. "You ever shot one before?"

"Yes." No. But right now was not the time to get into a debate about the similarities between blasters and the guns she'd done target practice with back home.

Her boss had wanted her competent in a whole slew of weapons, just in case she ran into trouble if she survived the wormhole. She'd long ago sold the armory he'd stocked her with. Earth goods were rare in space, and she had enough credits to be comfortable for a while.

Krax stared at her for several seconds before he shrugged, pulled his smallest blaster from a holster, and handed it over to her. Claudia took it and was surprised by the weight. She wrapped her fingers around the grip. It was more or less shaped like a pistol, though the barrel wasn't hollow. It would shoot a blast of energy anywhere she pointed it. They were non-lethal weapons, unless they were modified to be deadly.

She didn't feel any safer with the blaster in her hand, but she gave Krax a thankful nod and they walked on.

She didn't know how far they'd gone. Everything ached, partially from the way she'd been jostled from the crash and partially from the walk. Maybe if she had an idea of where they were going, the walk might not feel so useless.

Instead, she was following two practical strangers and hoping it turned out okay.

Something beeped and Seris held up a hand. They all stopped moving.

Krax and Seris moved to flank her, both of them peering into the jungle all around them. Claudia's heart started pounding again, and she wondered who the invisible monster was going to snatch this time. She gripped her blaster hard, but couldn't point it anywhere with Krax and Seris so close.

"Show yourself!" Krax demanded.

The jungle in front of him seemed to part, and four people stepped out, three men and a woman.

Her gaze immediately snagged on one of the men and her breath caught. He stared at them with the kind of intensity that exuded confidence, and then that intensity bloomed into a smile when he took the three of them in.

And that smile. Oof.

Handsome didn't cut it. He was the kind of hot that would stop traffic. Rock star hot. Model hot. Completely unattainable and somehow smiling at her in the middle of an alien jungle.

Claudia squeezed her eyes shut and looked at him again, certain she must have been hallucinating. But no, he was still there and still looked that damn good.

He wasn't the one who greeted them, though. That was the tall man in the center. "We picked up your distress signal. We're here to help."

THE HUMAN WOMAN looked small between the two mercs. She clutched an equally tiny blaster and was looking at him like she might need to use it. The urge to cross the distance, put an arm around her shoulders, clutch her close to him, and assure her that everything would be fine surged through him. Drake had to force himself to stay in one place.

How had a little human like her ended up huddled between two mercs? He doubted she was their prisoner. Mercs didn't usually give their prisoners blasters. And they were standing around her in a defensive posture.

Then he remembered the roster Fluke had found. Three mercs and a passenger. And the human was called Claudia.

"Who are you?" the male merc asked, scowling and jutting out his tusks.

Sentinel put a hand to his chest and gave a quick bow before making the introductions. The male merc introduced himself as Krax, the female was Seris, and they confirmed the human was Claudia.

"We explored the crash site and grabbed data from your ship. What happened to your fourth?" Sentinel asked. His eyes scanned the forest around them, looking for threats. All of them, dragons, merc, and human, were tense, and Drake didn't think it had anything to do with this unexpected meeting.

There was something out there. Somewhere.

"It happened fast," Krax reported. His hands tightened on his blast rifle before he took a deep breath and loosened his grip. "Whatever it was that took him, we couldn't see it. There was a flash of blood, a scream, and then it dragged him away so fast. I don't know if it was a person or an animal, but it was *smart*."

Distinctions between person and animal could get iffy when dealing with different alien species. But Drake understood what Krax meant.

"We need to find a safe place to park this one," he jerked his head toward Claudia, "then we're going hunting."

"Do you have a ship?" Seris asked. "Where are you

coming from?" She sounded calmer than her partner, but she was gripping her own blaster just as tightly.

"The ship is about fifty kilometers away," Sentinel reported. "And we're from Vemion. It's the closest planet in the system and the only one likely to have heard your distress call." Something snapped in the jungle around them and everyone froze. Sentinel and Fluke summoned their flames while Drake and Vise stepped closer to the others.

Claudia gasped and Krax growled while Seris stayed silent and watchful. They held their positions for at least a minute before beginning to breathe a little easier. Nothing rushed them, nothing attacked them. Whatever it was, it was a natural part of the forest and no immediate threat.

"It didn't make a noise before it took Ruzo," said Seris, shoulders visibly relaxing as she nodded to the dragons. "There's plenty of life in this jungle. We've been hearing it for hours."

The human clutched her blaster and eyed the dragons suspiciously for far longer than Krax and Seris did. He didn't know what made her do that, but his instinct to sidle up closer and promise to protect her until she was safely out of whatever danger this planet posed probably wasn't his smartest move. So Drake forced himself to stay where he was.

Sentinel and Fluke vanished their flames. "Do you

have any way to know if your man survived?" Sentinel asked. "Tracking beacons? Biodata?"

"No," Krax scowled. "We don't stay hooked into the computer during flight. Feels too invasive. Even if we did, all that data would be back on the flight computer. None of us have comms or any of our other equipment. We're flying blind. But we're not leaving him behind. Even if…"

No need to finish the sentence. A monstrous force had nabbed a trained mercenary like it was nothing. There was a good chance he'd be nothing but a pile of bleeding meat when they found him.

If they found him.

Drake's eyes snagged on Claudia's fingers as she slowly loosened her grip on her blaster. He should be keeping his eyes on the mercs who could actually pose a threat, but looking away was impossible. This must be terrifying for her. For anyone, but especially for a non-combatant who held a blaster more like a security blanket than a weapon.

"We're too far away to hike back to the ship," he said. Claudia already looked exhausted, her clothes plastered to her by sweat and her head hanging low. The mercs could handle a fifty-kilometer hike, but not the human. And Drake would offer to let her ride him in his other form before he asked her to make the trek. "We'll need to scout for a nearer landing spot and if it's safe, one of us can fly out and bring the ship closer. We should also establish a base while we look for Ruzo."

Sentinel gave him a look, the kind that meant they'd be having words later. "Yes," he agreed, voice a bit stilted. "Have you all been able to find a defensible resting place?"

Seris shook her head. "Haven't bothered looking. We wanted to get to higher ground and scope it out." She reached back and laid her hand on the pack sticking up over her shoulder. "We're not completely defenseless."

"Fluke, I want you in the air and scouting ahead. We'll go north a bit and see if we can find a place. Signal if you see anything."

Fluke took two running steps before launching himself at a vine and climbing up. He disappeared into the canopy, and a moment later Drake heard the flap of wings.

Claudia stared after him as if she expected something more and muttered to herself. It made no sense to Drake, and before he could ask her about it, they were moving on.

CHAPTER
SIX

IF CLAUDIA THOUGHT TOO HARD, everything was going to fall apart. She'd gotten used to the idea of aliens. It didn't even take that much brain wrangling. How could it when one of the first things that happened to her when she crawled out of her capsule was encounter a nine-foot tall, segmented, insect looking thing with over a hundred legs and a voice made for telling stories?

So, aliens. Right. Easy peasy.

Dragons, though. Dragons were something else.

There were legends about dragons back on Earth. And she'd basically thrown all the legends out. Aliens weren't giant green creatures interested in abductions and probes, at least not the ones she'd met. What would she encounter next? Werewolves? Vampires?

And would they be as hot as the dragon who kept eyeing her up?

After another arduous hour, they'd found a place the dragons and mercs had declared satisfactory. Claudia figured it had to do with the bend in a river near them and the way the trees acted as a wall. She would rather be able to see the bad guy coming, but she wasn't about to offer up her own ideas. She was pretty sure she was the only person on this mission without combat experience.

She was sitting with her back against her pack, blaster set on the ground beside her, and a canteen of water clutched in her hands. It was somehow still cool going down and was possibly the best thing she'd ever drank.

She only hoped it didn't end up being her last.

Krax and Seris had gone off with two of the dragons to look for Ruzo, leaving her with the sexy dragon and the girl dragon. Okay, she really had to learn names before she went any further, otherwise she was going to embarrass herself.

But to do that, she might need to take her eyes off the sexy one. He was tall, with dark hair and eyes made for sin. She'd caught him shooting grins at his fellow dragons and cracking jokes as they trekked through the jungle, trying to lighten the burden that was the hike.

Some jokesters could be really annoying about it, but not this guy. He made the steps a little easier to take, and carried his weight. He'd even offered to take her pack, but Claudia had insisted on doing her part. Of course, once they started climbing up a hill, she'd regretted it. But she would have cut her own tongue out rather than complain.

And now sexy dragon guy was looking at her. And grinning.

"I'm bad with names," she forced herself to admit. It was sort of true. Her tongue couldn't fit around some of the alien languages she'd encountered, even with the communicator she had. But mostly she'd been focused on staying alive when this guy's boss did the introductions, and she'd missed out on anything else.

And she'd been a bit focused on the dragon thing.

The guy smiled and laid a hand on his chest. "I'm Drake. Vise is the one doing the water testing by the river. Sentinel is the serious guy in charge. And Fluke is the frowny one, he's—" Drake bit his bottom lip and shook his head. "Never mind."

"Come on, tell me!" She found herself leaning forward, intrigued by whatever he wasn't saying.

But Drake just laughed a bit and shook his head. "Nah, Sentinel might throw me out the airlock if he hears I'm badmouthing his crew."

"Not your crew?" They'd been moving as a single unit. "Are you a passenger or something?" But that didn't make sense. They were coming from the nearby planet. Venom or something.

"Or something," Drake agreed. He shifted and scooted until he was sitting closer to her. "Are you cold?" he asked.

She'd been shivering. Only half of it was from fear. She'd dug a blanket out of her pack, but it wasn't doing much to keep her warm. And that seemed crazy, since they were in the middle of the jungle. She'd been covered in sweat earlier, but now it was drying and there was a faint breeze making her shake.

"I wish we had a warming block in our packs." She hunched into her blanket and pulled the sides closer together. It probably made her look a bit pathetic, but she'd do just about anything for warmth at the moment. She wondered if Drake might give her a cuddle.

The dragon grinned at her and held his hands in front of him. "I think I can do better than that." Fire burst from one hand and he threw it from one to the other like he was juggling.

It was so mesmerizing that Claudia let go of the blanket and sat up straighter until it fell off her shoulders, the chill momentarily forgotten. "You can just do that?" Some primitive part of her wanted to reach out and touch it, as if she'd forgotten that fire burned. "This is some trick, right?" Drake looked so human that she let herself forget he was an alien. A *dragon*. But here he was, summoning fire as if it was nothing.

Drake held out both hands palms up and let his fire hover above them. "Not a trick," he promised. He slid a little closer to her. "Is this warmer?"

She shivered, but this time it had nothing to do with the chill. He smelled clean with a hint of something earthy, all enhanced by the fire. She wanted to nuzzle up against him and let him take all her worries away.

But Claudia forced herself to stay exactly where she was, six important inches of space between them. She wasn't here to start relying on some random rescuer. She controlled her own fate. Yes, she and the crew she was with needed the help. But that didn't mean she was going to chase after more.

Instead, she focused on the fire. She let her hands hover near it and grinned up at Drake. "I wish I could do something like that," she admitted. She focused on the flame and the warmth sank into her skin until she felt more connected to that fire than any she'd ever felt before.

As she swayed in her seat, it seemed to move with her and then straighten again. Drake had to be doing it, playing with her and the fire at the same time. But she couldn't bring herself to care. She held a hand up near the fire and didn't warn him—she wanted to see what he'd do next. She shot her palm out and concentrated on the flame, thrusting out like she'd done as a child playing superheroes with the neighborhood kids.

The fire shot out of Drake's palm and hit a tree near them.

He yelped and jumped out of his seat. In a blink, the fire was gone and he was staring at her like she'd grown a second head.

Claudia laughed. "Holy crap, that looked awesome. Do you control it telekinetically?"

Drake flexed his hands, opening and closing his palms several times before he pulled them back in and laid them against the outsides of his thighs. "You... that's—"

Whatever he was about to say was cut off by the sound of a scream.

CHAPTER
SEVEN

DRAKE HAD to push every thought aside as he sprinted through the forest towards the aborted scream. It was the kind of scream a soldier rarely got to make as an enemy snuck up on them. But when it happened, there was no saving the soldier.

He wondered who it was and if they were going to find a body, or only more blood.

Even with the pressing need to speed up and investigate the problem, Drake tempered his speed. Claudia was right behind him and he wasn't letting her out of his sight.

Especially not now that she might be his mate.

He didn't waste time cursing his wayward brain as the things he was trying not to think about washed over him. She had taken control of his flame as if it belonged to her. There had been no breeze, no other force around them. Humans didn't have the kind of powers that would allow them to harness a dragon's flame.

Except for humans who were destined for dragons.

But how could it be? The matchmaker had been clear that he wouldn't find his mate. She'd all but dared him to do something extreme. Was she a fraud?

Or was she more right than he could imagine?

If he'd left Vemion to search for his mate, Sentinel wouldn't have asked him to come along on this rescue mission. If he'd sought her out, she would have been long gone before he returned to Vemion.

Or worse.

He didn't know how his family would react if he brought home a human mate, but he didn't care. He'd been looking for his mate forever, and now he would dedicate his life to keeping her.

But he had to keep her alive first.

And that meant he couldn't think about their bond. Not when the memory of a scream still hung in the air and there was some sort of monster outside hunting them.

He, Claudia, and Vise found the others on the edge of the river, a bit upstream from where they planned to camp. Seris, Krax, and Sentinel were there too.

There was no sign of Fluke.

Except for the puddle of blood Sentinel was

crouching over. It had splattered against a large rock, otherwise it might already have been absorbed into the soft soil under their feet. Drake quickly recalibrated the threat the monster posed to them. It was one thing to sneak up on a merc. But a dragon? He knew exactly how competent Fluke was. Besides, all dragons were living weapons. If he'd been taken with only enough time to scream, the monster was something to be feared.

Sentinel stood and looked at each of them before speaking. "Was anyone with Fluke when he was taken?"

Negatives all around.

Sentinel was braced for the information and took it like he'd been expecting it. He crouched back down again and kept studying the blood. He shuffled on his feet, following a trail that was too distant for Drake to make out.

Beside him, Claudia leaned towards him a bit and Drake shifted his weight so she could lean up against him if she chose. He wanted to be her tower of strength, but he got the idea she might reject it if he offered outright. She was a human alone on a merc ship, a passenger deep in the galaxy and far from home. She couldn't get this far by showing weakness.

But more than anything, he wanted to be her strength.

He had to bite back a smile when her fingers brushed his forearm and stayed there. She wasn't holding his hand. He wouldn't be surprised if she was making some sort of mental negotiation with herself that made it alright to touch his forearm but not his hand.

He'd take whatever he could get.

"The trail only goes a few meters," Sentinel said once he'd studied the blood for long enough. "It might have dragged Fluke into the river. Or it can teleport."

"If it can, we're fucked," spat Krax. "That's one of ours and one of yours. How long until it kills us all?"

"We don't know that they're dead," Seris tried to reason.

Krax scowled at her and seemed ready to show his disagreement with his fists.

But before he could do more than glare, Vise held up a small black device. "I'm having trouble getting a location, but Fluke's tracker shows he's alive. We'll know if he transitions from rescue mode to recovery mode."

They'd know if he died.

"Can the monster thing remove the tracker?" Claudia asked. She pulled her hand away from his arm and took a step to the side, standing completely on her own. "If I was an evil monster, I wouldn't want anyone hunting me down."

"We're using a chemical tracker," Vise explained. She stepped closer and showed the device to Claudia. "It'll be active for quite some time, or until we return home and take an agent that counteracts the tracker. As long as we're on this planet, we'll be able to track each other."

Claudia nodded her understanding and took a shaky breath, but she didn't speak further.

"From now on, no one goes anywhere alone," Sentinel declared.

"I'll stick with Seris," Krax said so quickly he must have thought Sentinel was going to designate the partnerships.

"I'm with you, boss," said Vise.

Claudia glanced at him with a shrug. "I guess that means it's me and you."

Drake nodded. He wasn't letting anything get to his mate. Not now, not ever.

CHAPTER
EIGHT

VISE AND SENTINEL were the only ones not in the camp. They'd decided to search out Fluke's signal by air. That left Claudia with Drake, Krax, and Seris. But she'd feel even safer if everyone was huddled around the fire.

Drake had set up barriers and pulled another fancy device out of his pack. This one set up a force field around their camp that should keep them safe from the monster. Claudia didn't know if she'd trust it enough to actually fall asleep, but it made her slightly less jumpy as they sat around the fire and ate the gross food from their packs.

For some reason, survival food was never tasty. Best case scenario, it tasted like cardboard. The nutrition bar she was eating now tasted like mud with weird little bumps in it.

Yuck.

But food was energy, and they were going to need it if they were going to find a way off this planet. She forced herself to chew and tried not to think about what kind of stuff could make the textures she was eating.

Bugs. It had to be bugs.

Claudia gagged but forced herself to swallow it all back down. She didn't want any food lingering in her mouth for longer than it had to. And she gulped down water from her canteen so quickly she risked giving herself a stomach ache.

Drake shot her a companionable grimace as he ate his own nutrition bar, and that made her feel a bit better. She tried to keep an open mind to food. She'd found dozens of dishes that she absolutely loved. But some things just tasted gross.

Drake finished off his nutrition bar with a flourish and winced so comically she almost burst out laughing. He leaned in conspiratorially. "When I was preparing for the academy, my brothers convinced me that I'd impress my instructors if I could eat these nutrition bars without reacting. Every day for a week, it was all I ate. I think I started to forget what good food actually tasted like. The family chef thought I was going to demand he be fired. And then Sentinel came to visit, saw what I was eating, and informed me that my brothers were playing a dirty trick. I apologized profusely to Chef, and we convinced him that Cipher and Storm were both undergoing a spiritual cleanse and could only eat unseasoned, boiled green vegetables for a month, and that he couldn't change their meals, even if they asked, because they'd asked me to ensure that they didn't stray from the path."

"Did it work?" she asked, though boiled, unseasoned green vegetables would taste a lot better than what she was currently eating.

"For about a week. Then our mother caught on and put a stop to it."

"So this was when you and your brothers were boys?" What did young Drake look like? She imagined a boy with mischief in his eyes and a completely innocent grin.

Drake burst out laughing. "Cipher was thirty! He's the eldest. Then there's Storm, then me. I was twenty at the time. About six years ago."

"Oh, so it's *that* kind of relationship." It sounded like something she'd see on a TV show. Her family had been too sedate for that. They loved each other, but in a quiet way. No need for pranks.

And definitely no chefs.

How rich was Drake if he was talking about a family chef like it was the most natural thing in the universe? Was the chef the only employee? Or had he grown up with dozens of servants and anything he wanted delivered on a silver platter? A man like that wouldn't need to sign up for a potential suicide mission in the hopes that the paycheck would cover his family's medical expenses.

It was one thing to be from different planets, but they really were from different worlds.

Before she could ask for more stories, Krax and Seris' voices rose above the fire, an argument brewing. "That's not the damned legend and you know it," Seris insisted. She was more heated than Claudia had ever heard her.

"I know what I'm talking about." Krax was resolute. "One of the guys on the crew worked with one of the survivors on a job a dozen years back. That's basically firsthand knowledge."

"That's secondhand at best," Seris corrected. "And if you're talking about Tisch, he's been drinking himself into a stupor every night for a decade and can't remember his own name half the time, let alone some ghost story he heard from an old buddy. We shouldn't be scaring ourselves with legends. We need to plan based on what we know. And, anyway, I heard it differently. From Vega, and she knows what she's talking about."

Krax scowled. "Vega? Did she hide in the shadows and let the monster eat everyone until she could kill it while it was distracted and take the bounty for herself?"

"That's not how she is. Don't listen to nasty rumors. You know her."

Drake must have had enough. "What are you two talking about?" he demanded. And she wasn't sure if it was her imagination, but it looked like smoke was wafting off of him.

It must have been the fire.

Then again, he was a dragon.

The smoke dissipated after a moment, and Seris nudged Krax to the side. "We've both heard stories of monsters that can't be seen."

Curiosity swirled within her, and it had little to do with the threat in the jungle. "Yeah? Tell us!"

Drake reached out and rested his hand on her arm, giving her a concerned look. "Are you sure? I don't want tonight to be even worse for you." His eyes were full of an emotion she couldn't read, and it made her heart flip over a bit.

God, what would it be like if he looked at her like that all the time?

Claudia forced herself to answer with a smile. "I love a good ghost story."

Krax and Seris had gone back to arguing under their breath, but after another prompt from Drake,

Krax began speaking. "This happened fifteen years ago—"

"Or possibly not at all," Seris interjected.

Krax cleared his throat and glared at her. "Anyway, it was on a planet like this. Dense jungle, no settlements. Easy pickings. The crew came in to collect some ore deposits and planned to be there a few weeks. This is the kind of job you dream about as a merc."

"You dream of it if you don't want action," Seris muttered.

"Or when you want easy credits," he corrected. "It's basically a vacation. Bots do most of the work. That's what the crew thought until one day, one of them went missing."

Anticipation sizzled up Claudia's spine as the story began to take shape. Even light years away from home, campfire stories had the same rhythm.

"They found blood and his fallen pack, but there was no trail, no hint of where he'd gone. That put the crew on edge. But it's a job and things happen. And the payday was too big to walk away just because one guy went missing. They worked through the day, drank through the night, and when they woke up the next morning, another crew member was gone."

"Yeah, yeah, yeah." Seris took over at this point.

"And they were all picked off one by one until Tisch ran home with a pile of ore and no other witnesses. Vega actually saw something. She was on a small crew, but the planet they went to was inhabited. The first night, the locals told them about the monster in the mountain. They called it a Shadowmorph. Anyone who climbed past a certain stream never came back, they were taken by the monster. But Vega and her crew had a mission to do, and they needed to get up the mountain. They didn't believe there was really some sort of unkillable monster up there, but they came armed for anything— motion sensors, heat sensors, stun nets, you name it, they were carrying it. It still nabbed their scout. But the rest of the crew kept moving. Slower, but moving. When they camped one night, she set up top of the line motion sensors. Even if the Shadowmorph only caused the leaves of the trees to move, it would catch it. And it did. In the middle of the night, the alarm blared and she caught sight of a beast, three meters tall. They blasted it with everything at hand, and it ran away. They decided the job wasn't worth it and ran for their ship. They never did figure out what happened to the scout."

Maybe ghost stories weren't what they should be telling. Claudia tried to imagine a three-meter tall monster and felt vaguely ill. That was as tall as an elephant. And not nearly as friendly.

But she refused to show her fear. She'd said it was

okay, and she had to make it through this. She was the civilian, the weak link, and she didn't want anyone judging her for that.

"I've got a story, though there's not any Shadow-morphs in it. It's about the most haunted day of the year and a summer camp where the blood runs freely..." She'd only started getting into the story when she heard a crack in the jungle behind her.

Claudia bit back a scream and spun, ready to face a three-meter monster with her bare hands.

CHAPTER
NINE

THE FORCE FIELD beeped as it recognized Sentinel and Vise, and Drake let out a ragged breath. All the talk of Shadowmorphs and summer camps was making him fear his own shadow, and he couldn't be doing that when there was a real monster out there.

The two dragons set their gear down near the fire and ensured that the force field was functioning properly before they sat down and took out their own nutrition bars. Sentinel ate his with a stoic face while Vise grimaced her way through every bite.

Drake could tell they had news from the swiftness with which Sentinel ate. Krax and Seris were both vibrating with the need for information on their side of the fire while Claudia was taking deep breaths beside him. He reached out and grabbed her hand, squeezing her palm. She squeezed back.

He wished he could use some sort of ancient magic to get her away from this place. He didn't want his mate near whatever monster—a Shadow-morph, perhaps—was hunting their group. No matter what, it was too dark now to do much. Moving would be more dangerous than staying within the force field.

Provided the Shadowmorph didn't know how to disable one.

Drake kept that doubt to himself. It was a sturdy device and nearly indestructible. He was letting his own fears get to him.

"Well," Seris finally prompted. "What did you see? Are they…?"

No one needed her to finish the question. Putting the words into the air was borrowing trouble.

Sentinel neatly folded the wrapper for his nutrition bar before sticking it in a pocket. "We had to fly high to get a good signal on our tracker. And even then, it was spotty at best. It directed us to a five-kilometer radius some distance from here."

"Did you find them?" Krax asked.

"We couldn't risk flying low," said Visc. "We don't know if this thing has the tech to shoot us out of the sky. The jungle is dense. But we did see what looked like smoke from a campfire in the same radius that's giving us Fluke's signal."

Krax jumped up. "Then let's go. We can't let that thing have them for another second."

Seris was slower to stand, but she joined her crew mate. "If Ruzo is out there, we need to find him," she agreed.

"That's suicide." Drake couldn't hold it back. The forest was pitch black around them, not even moonlight filtering in through the canopy. If it weren't for their fire, they wouldn't be able to see at all. Add in a monster that already seemed to be invisible, and Krax and Seris were walking into death.

"Your crew is out there too." Krax was adamant, already pulling on his bag.

"No one is leaving." Sentinel didn't yell. He didn't have to. He had the kind of command in his voice that made everyone freeze. He pierced Krax and Seris with a look. "Neither of you have trackers. If you get lost, we can't find you. It's too dark to find our people or investigate the site we think they might be at. We'll head out at first light for a better look. But we'll be no help to them if we kill ourselves tonight."

Krax breathed heavily and Drake wondered if he would do something stupid. But Krax just spat and stalked off until he could situate himself at the furthest reach of the force field, where he set down his things. A moment later, Seris joined him.

"We decided not to bring our ship in any closer," Vise said, as if two mercs hadn't just stalked off in a huff. "We don't want to put our only vehicle at risk."

Drake saw the logic, but he glanced at Claudia out of the corner of his eye. He wanted her on the ship, in all the comfort it could provide, and behind its considerably stronger defensive field. He wanted so much more, but he had to quash those desires.

At least until they were safe and he could invite her into his bed. His home. His life.

Forever.

Sentinel and Vise set up their own rest area which left him and Claudia alone. Well, as alone as they could be in a relatively small force field with four other people.

Claudia rested back on her elbows and the shadows of the fire danced over her. Drake couldn't resist sitting close. He wanted to offer her a spark of his flame, wanted to confirm that what he'd seen earlier hadn't been some trick. She'd controlled his fire.

She was his.

But Sentinel and Vise were nearby, and they'd know what he was doing. He had no intention of hiding his mate from the world, but that didn't mean he was ready to declare himself quite yet. And he didn't want Sentinel or Vise questioning his judgment when it came to Claudia.

"You're looking serious," she said. She raised her hand up for a minute, as if she planned to touch him before snatching her hand back and placing it back on the ground.

"It's a serious time," he said and then wanted to curse himself. What did that even mean? He knew how to talk to women, some might even say too well. So why did his brain stutter with this one? "What was that story you were telling?"

It was almost too dark to tell, but he thought she was blushing. "It wasn't real," she confessed.

"Yeah?" he leaned closer, and their shoulders brushed together. "What was it then?"

"*Friday the Thirteenth.*" She said it like it was supposed to mean something. She continued when Drake didn't have a response for that. "It's this old horror movie. A bunch of teenagers get hunted down one by one at a summer camp. I saw it once when I was a kid and had nightmares for a month." She shuddered. "It was my mom's favorite movie."

"You scare yourselves for entertainment?" He couldn't say he knew much about humans, even though two of his cousins had married them.

"I mean, maybe a little? You've never done

anything a little risky just for the exhilaration of it all?" Her shoulder brushed against his and stayed there. They were moving closer together and the rest of the camp might as well have not existed.

"Perhaps a time or two," he admitted. "But I'm a dragon, there's not much that puts me at risk." She didn't respond to that, and Drake got the feeling he'd misstepped. "How did you leave Earth?" he asked to change the subject. "I thought your planet wasn't yet in contact with other planets."

"How do you know about Earth? We're not space-famous, are we?" Her eyes brightened, and she grinned at him.

Stars above, if they were alone, he'd taste that grin.

"My cousin's mate is from Earth. Courtney. She was abducted and he rescued her." And by bringing her back, he'd rocked the expectations of dragon society. Crux was a prince, heir to the throne. And now his queen wouldn't be a dragon.

"I wasn't abducted. Does that really happen?" The space seemed to keep shrinking between them, and he wondered if he could just pull her on top of him.

But no, restraint was needed. He was a lord and a warrior. He had restraint.

He still couldn't stop himself from trailing his

fingers over the back of Claudia's hand until she shivered from nothing that had to do with the cold.

"It happens," he confirmed. "Most of the humans you run into in the galaxy were either abducted from Earth or are descendants from abductees. In other cases, someone crash landed on your planet and agreed to take some humans back with them."

"Is there some sort of galactic agreement not to contact planets that can't do major space travel or something? You know, there's actually a theory like that back home, or maybe I'm getting it confused with *Star Trek*. But I've definitely heard of it." She flipped her hand over so their palms pressed together.

Drake's mind threatened to go haywire from that simple touch. This was a special kind of torture, and he didn't want to escape. "Earth is out of the way of most populated systems. I think that's why you've been left alone."

She made a face. "Well, that's kind of boring. I don't think humans will be stuck on our little rock for much longer. I ended up this far away because I signed up to be an experiment. My boss wanted to send someone through a wormhole. I was pretty sure I wasn't going to make it, but there was this tiny chance I'd get to explore the universe in a way no human ever had. Or, I guess, no human had ever really gotten to choose to. He gave me a ton of training and my family got an ungodly amount of money. About three years ago, Earth years, I mean, I got strapped onto a rocket and blasted off. I must have had the angels smiling down on me. I landed on a small inhabited planet and met my first aliens. Since then, I've been exploring."

"You're amazing." Unbidden, the memory of his most recent lady love came back to him. He tried to banish it, her disappointment at his less than exciting life.

She'd only wanted him to fight a duel. Claudia had jumped into a wormhole without knowing if she'd come out the other side.

What would she think when she found out he didn't spend most of his days running from monsters and rescuing mercenaries?

"I'm not anything special." She was shaking her head and looking away. "I just got lucky. Or maybe I was the only one stupid enough to take the job."

She tried to shift away, but Drake reached out and stopped her. He didn't hold her tight, didn't want to force her into anything, but that simple touch was enough to freeze her in place.

Their eyes met and a connection sizzled between them. Her tongue darted out to lick her lips, and Drake had to bite back a groan as the imagined feel of it went straight to his cock. He'd been able to focus on anything but his own body until now.

And now he wanted with a fierceness that shocked him.

He leaned in, desperate for just a taste. Surely that much would be allowed. And he thought he saw Claudia leaning in right back.

Then the scream had to ruin everything.

CHAPTER
TEN

SOMEHOW SHE'D FORGOTTEN about the threat. Only for a few seconds, but long enough that the scream seemed to come out of nowhere. Then her memories of the rest of the day, and all the aches and pains in her body that she'd been ignoring, came roaring back.

Oh hell. She was on some monster planet and an invisible thing was hunting them.

Had an hour of flirtation really banished that all away?

Claudia chased after Drake to the other side of their camp and was shocked at the state Seris was in. She hadn't known the merc for long, but every time they'd met, Seris had been nothing but put together. Now her eyes were wild and her voice hoarse as she sobbed out what she'd just seen.

"Krax... gone." She sucked in one breath and then another, and they steadied her. If Claudia knew her a bit better, she might have offered support, but she was pretty sure Seris would take offense to that.

"He stepped just behind those bushes to take a piss," Seris said, voice clearer now. "I could see his shoulders, even with the dark. Then something rustled in the leaves and between one blink and the next, he was gone."

Claudia couldn't make out the spot Seris was talking about. The force field made the air in front of them shimmer a bit, and the world around them was way too dark to see without a flashlight.

"We have a spot dug out to take care of that." Sentinel's words teetered on the edge of anger, but he pulled himself back. "I want everyone by the fire. Now. No going outside the force field, no walking anywhere alone."

"But Krax—"

Sentinel cut her off. "We're not going after him tonight. And we're not going to talk about our plans at all if there's a chance that thing is lurking."

Seris looked ready to stomp off into the darkness to find her partner, but the fire went out of her after a minute, and her shoulders slumped. She shuffled back to the fire with the rest of them.

Claudia should have been tired. As she settled

back into her seat, though with a bit of distance from Drake this time, she was determined to fall asleep. The only thing that would make tomorrow any worse was if she had to face it with the weight of exhaustion trying to drag her down.

Sleep didn't come.

Of course it didn't. How could it when she was certain that if she closed her eyes for too long everyone around her would disappear?

She tried every trick she knew. She even resorted to counting imaginary sheep. She got to three hundred and seventy-three before she decided all that was doing was making her anxious about losing count.

She really could have used a sleeping pill, but didn't even consider asking for one. She was already the biggest liability among them, and needing to be carried because she was in a drugged stupor would make everything even worse.

Drake's even breathing teased her ear, and she looked over at him. His chest rose and fell in a comforting rhythm. She wanted to demand to know his secret. There was a monster out there! How could he sleep?

But some people were just like that.

And she'd never been able to fall asleep easily. Even when there weren't any monsters.

Watching his chest rise and fall was comforting in

its own way. Claudia let herself be entranced by it and slowly, achingly and impossibly slowly, her eyes drifted shut.

The sleep wasn't peaceful. She rose to half-consciousness more than once, often when Seris or the dragons switched off the watch. But even when Drake rose to do his shift, he didn't move away from her.

Claudia couldn't get used to him. He was going away as soon as they were safe.

But for right now, she'd cling to the way he made her feel.

She blinked awake for good just as the sun was starting to trickle through the canopy overhead. Who knew what time it really was. Time didn't matter on a place like this. It wasn't like she had anywhere to be.

"I don't care! Two of my people are out there. I need to come with." Seris' voice wiped the last vestiges of sleep off of her. She sat up and saw Drake beside her. He gave her a look she couldn't easily interpret and shook his head minutely when she shifted to get to her feet.

She stayed put.

"We don't have the proper equipment for that, and we can't risk you falling off." The explanation came from Vise. "Carrying a person means flying a lot slower and lower than we're capable of. We can't do it."

"Then I'll follow on foot. Two of my men are out there. I'm not going to sit idly by and let them…" She sucked in a breath. "I need to find them."

"We can't leave—" Suddenly their voices got quieter, and Claudia knew they must be talking about her.

She didn't need to hear them to know what they were saying. Seris and Drake needed to guard Claudia.

Claudia was their biggest liability. Yes, Seris couldn't fly or shapeshift into a giant dragon, but she was an experienced mercenary. She could climb up to the monster's lair and fight it with her bare hands.

Or maybe not.

After all, the monster had already taken two experienced mercenaries and a dragon. Maybe no person, no matter how experienced, was a match for that thing.

Shadowmorph. That was what they had called it in the story. Was *that* what was hunting them? Was this its territory?

Claudia's stomach roiled. She wished she could go home. At least there she understood the monsters that she would be facing. At least she would see a bear coming. And bears didn't hunt people or kidnap them.

What if they weren't facing a monster at all? What if they were facing some kind of person who had gone a bit crazy and was now using this jungle planet as his hunting ground?

She turned her attention away from Seris' protests. She wasn't in charge of that, and frankly she didn't want to be.

It didn't take very long for Sentinel and Vise to launch themselves into the air, leaving Claudia, Drake, and Seris behind. Seris glared at her and Drake and then stomped off to the farthest corner of the encampment. She pointedly turned her back on Claudia and Drake.

Claudia shot Drake a look.

He shrugged.

What more was there to say? Seris would have to get over it. And if all went well, her comrades and Fluke would be rescued in just a few hours.

Or maybe they would know for sure that they weren't coming back.

Claudia finally threw off the rest of the makeshift blanket she'd slept in and looked around for anything she could use to clean up. Just wiping her face off would make her feel ten times cleaner.

Drake handed her a canteen sloshing with water. "We filled up our water supplies this morning. Too bad we can't ensconce the stream in our force field. And there's a little dugout over there." He nodded towards a section of the force field camp that was hidden behind some reclaimed branches and offered about as much privacy as anyone could have in such a small space. "You can head there if you need to take care of any business."

Right. Bathrooms were a luxury.

She was never traveling off the beaten path again.

But a few minutes later, Claudia was as washed and refreshed with personal business as she could expect to be. Drake handed her a nutrition bar and she choked it down, trying to ignore the nasty taste. She missed food. And a bed. And shelter.

Camping sucked.

Seris was still sitting off to the side and staring into the burbling stream just beyond the force field as if it offered her answers to questions that Claudia didn't know she was asking.

The morning progressed, and it soon became apparent there wasn't much to do. Survival packs weren't exactly flush with entertainment material, and Claudia could only do so many laps around their camp before she had memorized every landmark they had erected. Drake was sitting on the same log he had been sitting on all morning and watching her as she moved.

"What?" she finally asked when she couldn't stand another moment of it.

"I can't watch you?" He grinned at her. And was

she imagining it, or was that a flirtatious tone in his voice?

Maybe he was just doing it to get her mind off the monster in the jungle. Or maybe he was just a flirtatious guy. But what would a mighty dragon want with a plain old human?

Or was she just getting her ideas from stories she had heard back on Earth, *Star Trek* and all those other shows her mother had watched on afternoon television.

Could Drake actually be flirting with her? Did he possibly want something that went beyond however long this rescue mission would take?

Did she care? Even if this was just blowing off steam, she definitely had steam to blow off.

"I guess you can watch me, if I can watch you." She grinned right back at him.

He held out his palm, and a moment later fire flickered up from it.

Claudia's breath caught. He did it as naturally as breathing. Well, she supposed, it would be natural for him, even if it was still something amazing to her.

"Do you want to try something?" he asked.

That was the kind of question that could lead a girl into trouble. "Try what?"

He tossed the flame between his hands and her

eyes followed back and forth, mesmerized. "Do you want to try?"

"I don't want to get burned." It was one thing to watch, but she wasn't crazy enough to stick her hand into fire on the promise of one hot guy.

Was she?

"Do you trust me?" Somehow, the question was more intimate than it should have been, something he might have asked if they were alone in his bedroom.

In his bed.

She wanted to say yes. She had no reason not to trust him. After all, he and his team had traveled across the universe—or at least a solar system—and were in the process of saving her life. He hadn't done anything to show that he was untrustworthy.

"Why?" When in doubt, stall. It had gotten her out of more than one sticky situation.

"Hold out your hand," he commanded. And then he raised his eyebrows in challenge when she didn't immediately do it.

Aw, hell. Just like that, he had her pegged. She couldn't resist a challenge. After all, it was a certain kind of person who would launch herself into space on the vague promise that she might survive the trip.

She held her hand out.

Drake was still sitting on the log, and he tossed a ball of fire right at her. Claudia flinched, but she kept herself in place. Either she was about to get inciner-ated or she was about to learn a super cool trick.

The fire landed in her palm, and though it tickled, it didn't burn.

She stared down at it until her eyes started to water and then looked over at Drake, the grin on her face huge. "What the hell? How is this possible?"

"Control it." He wasn't smiling. His face had gone utterly serious, and there was a rough undercurrent to his voice.

It made part of her want to toss the fire back to him and tell him that she didn't take orders. But this wasn't the kind of order that a person gave when they thought they controlled someone else. This was the kind of command that came out of desperation.

But why would she make him desperate?

Without any idea on how to actually control the flame, Claudia simply did what she had seen Drake do. She tossed the fire from one hand to another, choking back a gasp of surprise as it worked.

When she looked back up at Drake, he was stand-ing. She grinned at him and threw the ball of flame up into the air before catching it like it was a baseball.

Elation soared through her. This might have been the coolest, or maybe the second coolest after finding out aliens actually existed, thing to ever happen to her. A dragon was letting her play with his fire. She didn't know how it worked. She didn't know if it would start to burn her at some point. But it was super cool.

And then Drake had to go and drop playing with his fire to number three on the list because he strode forward, slid his hands through her hair, and covered her lips with his own.

CHAPTER
ELEVEN

DRAKE DIDN'T MEAN to kiss his mate. He didn't plan it. He knew he shouldn't. But as she tossed his fire back and forth as if she had been born to do it, the primal urge to claim her could not be resisted. In two strides, he covered the distance between them, and then his lips were on hers, swallowing up her gasp and then tasting her moan. Her hands gripped him close as their tongues tangled and Drake's body roared to life with desire.

He wanted to lift her up, to feel her legs wrapped around his waist as he drove into her over and over again. He wanted to hear her cry out his name as he took her to the peaks of pleasure. He wanted to claim her right then so that she knew that there would never be anyone else.

It was overwhelming. Exhilarating.

Perfect.

And from the way Claudia was kissing him back, she must have felt it too. She couldn't have known what it meant. Perhaps he should have told her. One day he would.

But not now, while the taste of her was imprinting itself on him, never to be forgotten.

They were alone in their own little world. The dangers around them melted away. Monster? What monster?

He and Claudia had each other and that was all that they needed.

He wanted to lay her out on the small makeshift bed she had made for herself last night, but some small bit of sanity interceded and he forced himself to pull away.

For one moment.

When he got a good look at Claudia, her cheeks were flushed and her eyes wide. Her wet and swollen lips pulled back into a grin, and before she could even say anything, he was kissing her again.

It was what he was made to do. She was his mate, after all. And he would prove to her that he was exactly what she needed.

He lost himself in the taste of her. They might have gone at it for minutes or for hours. Time didn't matter in the jungle. He only knew that he wanted, no, needed, more time with her.

His body was desperate for more, hard and screaming for attention. Claudia's hands teased their way under his shirt, tracing over his muscles and finally flirting with the waistband of his pants.

Drake groaned against her. Yes, this was what he needed. Hands on him. His mouth on her. Everything.

But something tickled the far edge of his consciousness. Something that made him pull back from the kiss and trap Claudia's hand against him before she could delve any deeper into his pants. He ached for the touch of her, but there was something he was forgetting.

He heard a sound, though he couldn't exactly say what it was.

He finally pulled away and turned just as Sentinel and Vise were entering the camp.

Both dragons gave him a look; there was no way to disguise what he and Claudia had just been doing. And Drake felt no shame. She was his mate. It was only natural. The dragons were lucky they hadn't arrived ten minutes later. Then they would get a real show.

Though that made a growl catch in the back of his throat. He didn't want anyone else seeing Claudia in that kind of position. She was his to claim, his to protect.

"Where's Seris?" Sentinel asked, eyes still darting between Drake and Claudia.

"Seris?" Had he forgotten about the other person in the camp already? He'd been so focused on Claudia and so sure that Seris could take care of herself that he hadn't given her a single thought since the argument that morning. He looked over to where she'd been sitting, staring off into the stream. Unsurprisingly, her seat was empty. He and Claudia were the only two people in the camp.

"Seris is gone?" Claudia stepped to the side of him so that she could see Sentinel and Vise for herself. "She was just there."

"Just there *when*?" asked Vise. "We've been gone for a while."

Claudia bit her swollen bottom lip and didn't answer. She couldn't. After all, Drake knew just how obsessed he'd been with her and all her attention had been on him. Neither of them knew when Seris had walked away.

Or been snatched.

Shame crashed over Drake. He had been brought on this mission to assist Sentinel, Vise, and Fluke. Now all three mercenaries were gone, along with

Fluke. And he had been so obsessed with tasting Claudia that he hadn't been doing his job.

He forced himself not to look at his mate. He wanted to reach out and touch her, to convince himself and her that this would all turn out well. Everything would be fine. Then he could take Claudia back home and show her his planet. Show her his estate. Ask her to stay.

But he couldn't do any of that until they were safe from the monster. And he would not touch her again until the job was done.

It was a sacred vow he made to himself. A vow that he knew he shouldn't break, even as he feared that he would.

But no, he had to keep it. He had a duty to see this job out. And duty had to supersede his wants. Even a want as big as claiming his mate.

He stepped away from Claudia and closer to Sentinel and Vise. "I don't know if she walked away or if she was taken," he admitted. "She was very angry this morning, but she didn't seem stupid. She wouldn't walk outside the protection of the force field."

"What if she saw Krax out there? Or thought she did?" If Claudia noticed the distance between them, she didn't comment on it. "Maybe she thought he'd been injured last night and she got sight of him. Or maybe the monster can duplicate our voices. It could have lured her out there."

He and the others considered it, though there was no way to prove it. Seris was gone. They had no way to track her. But they knew they were being hunted, and the thing hunting them could have easily lured her out if Claudia was right.

Drake feared she was.

"Any sign of camp?" Drake asked Sentinel.

"We flew a bit lower this morning," he confirmed. "No fire this time, but we got closer to Fluke's signal. I think we know where they are."

"But we don't know what state the others are in," Vise reminded them. "Getting them out could be an issue. Especially if…" Her eyes darted to Claudia and back.

Especially if Claudia was with them, he silently finished her sentence. Claudia was the liability. They couldn't rescue the others if they were trying to keep her safe.

He didn't want to separate from her. He wanted her right by his side so he knew that she was safe. But that kind of thought was the mate bond talking. Now he had to think like the dragon lord.

"We should take you back to the ship," he told Claudia, trying to sound like there was no room for argument. "The defenses are greater than the force field here. And if you're safe, we can go and face the monster."

"*No.*" The denial was emphatic. "You want to seal me up in a ship that I don't know how to fly while you guys go out and fight a monster that you can't even see. What if you all get killed?" Her eyes met his. "What if *you* get killed?"

Drake could feel a fist squeeze around his heart. Whatever he was feeling, she was feeling too. Or at least some version of it, even if she did not understand the mate bond. She knew there was something between them.

Given that kiss, how could she not?

The coward inside of him wanted to reassure her that all would be well. It was all he would need to say to get her to agree to go. But he would not lie about this, not to his mate.

Sentinel and Vise stayed quiet. It was obvious that he was the only one that could convince Claudia to go back to the ship.

He had to put any soft feelings aside and focus on the facts. "The ship has an autopilot feature. I can show you how to engage it. It will take you back to my home planet and you can get help there. All you have to give us is three days. If we're not back by then… Well. If we're not back by then, you should leave."

She leveled a look at him that bordered on a glare. "You want me to leave you behind? What if you just get bogged down?"

"We all have trackers," he explained. "If they're still showing us as alive, a bigger team can come to rescue us. And you can explain more about what they'll be facing. Trust me." Despite the seriousness of the situation, he couldn't help the grin that tugged at his lips. She had trusted him before. Maybe she would again. "Sentinel, Vise, and I are all trained dragon warriors. We can handle ourselves. So let me take you back to the ship and let us finish up this mission." The sooner it was done, the sooner they could go home. And he was going to have her in his bed. No matter what.

He had to keep his promises to himself. No matter how much he wanted to make it, he couldn't say them out loud. Not until this was done.

Claudia stared at him for several seconds as if she was trying to define some kind of hidden truth. Whatever she was looking for, she must have found it. Or given up. She gave a precise nod. "How do we get back to the ship?"

"We fly."

CHAPTER
TWELVE

CLAUDIA DIDN'T WANT to run and hide. But it wasn't like she wanted to fight the monster either. Really, all she wanted to do was cuddle up with Drake and explore every inch of him. Twice. And then she was going to do it all over again. She had a feeling each time she'd find something new.

He certainly wasn't like anyone she'd ever wanted before. And that had nothing to do with the fact that she was currently clenching her legs against his scales as he flew through the air in his dragon form, taking her towards his ship with Sentinel and Vise flanking them.

When he suggested flying, she hadn't immediately realized what he meant. Then her brain quickly caught up, and she'd been excited enough that she forgot for the moment why she needed to retreat.

She was getting to fly on a dragon's back. No one at home had ever done *that* before.

And few people at home would want to. Especially without any sort of harness keeping them in place. One wrong move would send Claudia plummeting to the ground, and there would be no need for a monster to finish her off. But she felt strangely secure seated as she was. It wasn't like a plane ride or anything like that. Maybe it was a bit like a hang glider, but she had never flown in one of those before, so she couldn't be sure.

It was an experience she would want to repeat over and over again, if she had the chance.

How are you doing? Drake's voice echoed in her head, and it made Claudia jolt, but not so badly that she lost her balance.

"What?" She asked it out loud, but it was swallowed by the wind around her. *What?* She asked it again, but intentionally projecting the thought with her mind. *How?*

Something like a chuckle echoed in her head. *We can talk this way,* Drake said, though he didn't explain it further. *How are you doing?*

I'm hanging on. Holy crap. Not only had she gotten to juggle a dragon's fire, not only had she gotten to kiss a dragon, now she was talking telepathically with one? How was this even her life?

We've only got about ten more minutes of flying, Drake explained. *Then you'll be safe in the ship.*

Claudia squeezed her eyes shut, trying not to let an errant thought loose. She was trying not to think of what came after the shields went up on the ship. Yeah, she would be safe. But what about the others? She really didn't want to consider what would happen to them.

They were going to be safe. She fixed that thought in her mind and made it her north star. It had to be true. She might have just met Drake, but there was something important about him. She wanted to see where the sparks between them would lead. And they couldn't lead anywhere if some sort of invisible monster ended up killing him before they really began.

They flew for a few more minutes, and Claudia was starting to think that they had gotten lucky. They were going to land shortly and at least she would be safe, even if she didn't really want to be the only safe person.

That was the moment that Vise screamed.

A dragon's roar went up and threatened to explode Claudia's eardrums. Her head whipped around and she saw Vise falling out of the sky, with Sentinel following her.

Drake picked up speed, but he wasn't following the falling dragons.

"What are you doing? Where are we going?" The questions came out of her mouth and her mind.

Need to get you to safety. Drake's mental voice was insistent.

"I can hold on," she insisted. *"That thing is out there. We have to chase after it."*

Drake didn't respond, and she was sure he was going to ignore her.

Then his voice echoed in her head. *Hold on.*

Then he jerked around and dove.

———

Drake knew that his first duty was to get Claudia to safety. Diving like this meant that he put her at risk, but he didn't dive as steeply as he would have in other circumstances. And she didn't falter. Of course she wouldn't. She was right where she belonged. And even if she didn't know it, she was built for this.

He couldn't leave Sentinel and Vise alone. Not if the monster was out there. Not if they were going to stand a chance against it.

He landed carefully and let Claudia climb off of him before shifting between forms. Sentinel had already shifted. There was no sign of Vise. Drake's eyes raked over the area around them. She couldn't just disappear like that. And how could it take out a fully shifted dragon?

He felt a flare of his flame, but he wasn't the one controlling it. Claudia summoned it and shot a burst of fire into the shadows. Something screamed.

The three of them ran towards it, Claudia pulling on his fire all the while as if she had been training with it for years.

A few meters out, there was a trail of smoke and the scent of singed flesh in the air.

But there was no monster. And no Vise.

The three of them stopped their run as the jungle threatened to close around them.

But unlike the last times the monster had claimed its victims, this time they had evidence of it. A smoking panel of what looked like high tech armor lay on the ground, scorch marks from Claudia's fire showing exactly where she had hit it even if she hadn't been able to see it.

Sentinel crouched over it and studied it for a moment before picking it up. "I've seen this before. This kind of armor has a built-in invisibility setting. That's why we can't see him. And it's almost certain to start malfunctioning now." He nodded towards

Claudia before looking back at Drake. "Your mate did well."

Drake couldn't help but smile.

But Claudia's face was a mask of confusion. "Mate?"

CHAPTER
THIRTEEN

DRAKE COULD SEE the moment that Sentinel's meaning washed over Claudia. He braced himself against the incoming questions and tried not to think destructive thoughts towards one of his oldest friends. They were in the middle of the jungle. There was an invisible monster hunting them. He didn't have time for this conversation.

Claudia's brow furrowed and she stared at him, definitely waiting for him to say something. He had to explain it. He'd been waiting for the right moment, but now maybe there was no right moment. Maybe he had to take whatever opportunity was presented to him and just go for it.

That was the plan, at least until he heard something crashing through the jungle near them.

Drake spun around, putting himself in front of

Claudia and any danger that might be coming their way. Was the monster coming back to finish them off? Or maybe Vise had somehow fought her way free of it and was going to find them.

He wanted to hope. He wanted *that* to be the truth. But he feared the worst.

Any blaster strong enough to bring a dragon down from flight would wreak havoc on them. Vise wouldn't be in fighting condition for some time.

Drake summoned his fire and held it in both hands, ready to strike.

A tall alien with tusks, his clothes torn to bits, burst out of the trees.

But it was Claudia who stopped him from firing on the man.

"Ruzo!" She clamped her hand down on Drake's shoulder and squeezed. "That's Ruzo. The first guy the monster took."

Ruzo was in bad shape. His face was a mess of cuts, bruising, and swelling, and one of his tusks was sitting at the wrong angle. His clothes looked like he had lost a fight with a bunch of knives, and he was panting. He looked like he had run a hundred kilometers, and he was holding himself so tightly that he had to be in great pain.

Neither Drake nor Sentinel vanished their flame. He didn't want to attack an escaped man, but this could be a trap. Perhaps the monster could change its form. Or perhaps he had done something to Ruzo to turn him into an enemy.

Drake had heard of control chips that slavers used to keep their people in line. They were disgusting devices, and his uncle, the King of Vemion, did his best to make sure that slavers and all of their trade stayed far away from Vemion, but there was always smuggling.

"You're Ruzo?" asked Sentinel, taking a cautious step towards the man.

Ruzo gave a tight nod, and at his side his hands curled into fists, as if he needed that extra sensation to keep himself standing.

Sentinel offered him a canteen and Ruzo took it gratefully, drinking in huge gulps. After only a moment, Sentinel tugged it away. "Take your time on that. Otherwise you're going to throw it back up."

Ruzo growled, but he didn't reach for the canteen again.

Drake focused on the jungle around them. He could hear the sound of insects and birds, the normal pace of life on this strange little planet. He didn't think the monster was hovering close, just waiting to pick them off. Not right now.

He hoped for all of his considerable worth that he was right.

"How did you find us?" That question came from Claudia, and she took two steps out from behind Drake so she could see Ruzo better.

Ruzo looked at her and seemed to relax a fraction. "He hasn't gotten you yet. Good." The words were rough, like he was speaking around glass that had been shattered in his throat.

"Not yet," Claudia confirmed, with fierce defiance. Not towards Ruzo, Drake knew, but towards the thing that was hunting them all.

Ruzo nodded again. "The other one. Your guy. He worked on my ties all night." Ruzo held up his hands, and they could all see the blistered skin around his wrists where something had once bound him. Fluke's flame had done a number on him, but he was moving. He lowered his hands. "That thing broke his leg. He couldn't run. But he got me out. And he gave me this." Ruzo reached into a pocket and pulled out a slim black device.

Drake recognized it as the same tracking unit that he and Sentinel were both carrying. Vise would have one on her as well. It allowed them to search for each other in an emergency.

"I've been trying to get to you all morning," said Ruzo. He was starting to tremble now, and Drake didn't know how much longer he'd last. "You were moving too fast, but I was going the same direction. It was my only choice. And then you stopped. I started running and I found you."

"When did you get free?" Sentinel asked.

It was a good question. He didn't mention Seris or Krax. Was the monster keeping them in different places? Or, even worse, was there more than one monster?

"That thing has been gone all day," Ruzo reported. "He left in the middle of the night last night. I took off as soon as my hands were... Well. As soon as it stopped hurting enough so that I could move."

Drake didn't want to consider just how much it would hurt to have a dragon lay his flame systematically against his skin until he could destroy the rope or chain or whatever it was that bound Ruzo. But the man was surviving for now, and they had to get him back to the ship before his injuries caught up with him.

"We need you to tell us everything you know about the monster's domain." That came from Sentinel, and Drake couldn't agree more.

Ruzo nodded. He opened his mouth to speak, but the only sound that came out was a groan. Then his eyes rolled back in his head and he collapsed to the ground.

THE REST of the flight back to the ship went as fast as they dared. Claudia was riding on Drake while Sentinel carefully clutched Ruzo in his claws. It was a precarious position, but they only had a dozen or so kilometers to cover, and they were back at the ship in no time. Sentinel rushed Ruzo to the med bay while Drake engaged the defensive system. He pointed Claudia toward the galley and asked her to investigate the food supply.

Neither he nor Sentinel would have time to eat before they left again, but he had a feeling that his mate would want something to do. And he wanted to know that she and Ruzo would have enough food if things went poorly.

By the time he headed toward the med bay, Sentinel already had Ruzo hooked up to the med bot, and there were a bunch of readings on the screen of the tablet that Sentinel was holding. "Mostly just dehydration and exhaustion," Sentinel informed him as he scrolled through the readings. "The trauma is nearly all superficial. He should be good after a few hours on the machine."

That was a relief. The monster had had Ruzo for longer than anyone else, and if he wasn't in terrible shape, there was a good chance that the others might still be alive. Or had the monster discovered Ruzo's escape and taken his wrath out on Fluke?

He and Sentinel would know soon enough.

Drake shouldn't be borrowing trouble.

"You didn't tell her." The change of subject was a punch to the gut.

Drake's head snapped up, and he stared at Sentinel as if the other dragon had just cursed out his mother. Though Drake doubted that even the king was brave enough to do that.

Sentinel was unrepentant. "We can't be keeping secrets on a mission like this. At least not secrets that will alienate people we're trying to help. Why are you stalling? Is it because she's human?"

Flame was in Drake's hand before he could even think to summon it and he could feel the smoke emanating off him. "How dare you." But he forced himself to release the flame. He wasn't about to attack

Sentinel with an injured Ruzo right there. He shouldn't attack Sentinel at all.

"I wanted to wait until things were a bit more settled. I'm not stalling." A mate was all he'd ever wanted, and the more he got to know Claudia, the more he desired her. It wasn't just the mate bond. She was exciting, and beautiful, and brave. Everything he could want in a partner. And the memory of that kiss still made him dizzy.

As if he would reject a mate just because she wasn't dragon. What kind of man would he be then?

Sentinel held up a pressure injector. "I'm going to wake him up. We need to hear what he has to say about what we're walking into."

Ruzo wouldn't want a lot of people to see him in such a vulnerable state. Sentinel was more than equipped to interrogate him alone. "I'll go show Claudia how to engage the autopilot. Just in case they need to leave without us."

Just in case we're dead, was what he really meant.

Sentinel gave him a nod and Drake left him to question Ruzo alone.

Drake found Claudia in the galley, exactly as he expected. She was scanning through their food processor, an impressed look on her face. He must have made a noise when he came into the room since her gaze snapped to him as soon as his shadow darkened the door.

"Some of these meals actually look *good*," she said with a grin and a pat of her stomach. "Most merc ships run on protein sludge and nutrition bars." That transformed her grin into a grimace.

"I think you've been traveling with the wrong mercenaries." Drake grinned back. Even in the darkest of times, smiling with Claudia felt right. "Sentinel has always liked a good meal. I'm pretty sure that once he retires from this," he made a circle with his hand to indicate the ship and the life that came with it, "he plans to open a restaurant back home. Or at least to invest in them. I wouldn't be surprised if he's journeying across the galaxy just to taste as many different cuisines as he can."

She brushed her finger over the screen and turned it off. "Well, it looks like we won't starve."

An awkward silence hung between them. He needed to explain about the mate bond. He shouldn't walk away without letting Claudia know exactly who she was to him. But if she didn't know and something went wrong, perhaps it wouldn't hurt her as bad.

One day she might recover.

It was one thing to lose a man you'd spent a day flirting with. It was quite another to lose your fated mate.

"I promise we'll talk when we get back," he said. It was the most he could do to acknowledge the bond between them without actually acknowledging it.

"You're leaving so soon?" Claudia rested her hand on the counter under the food processor screen. Her knuckles whitened as she gripped the edge tightly. "Maybe we should just call for reinforcements now that we have the defenses up."

He wished they could. "The others are still alive," he said. "There's no guarantee that will be the case by the time reinforcements get here."

He didn't want to walk off and leave his mate alone—well, mostly alone. He didn't want to face an invisible monster with only Sentinel as backup. But this was his duty. He'd come to this planet to rescue people and he would do it.

Claudia let out a shaky breath and gave him a tight nod. "If that's what you have to do."

"It's not like this all the time," he said and hoped it was enough to reassure her. "I don't usually run head-first into danger."

Her tension didn't ease, but she nodded again. "That's good to hear."

Everything had been so easy back at their camp. Too easy, really. After all, their distraction had led to Seris being taken. But Drake wanted that easy camaraderie back. "We're going to have a conversation," he promised again. "I'll tell you everything. We'll be back in no time."

Now it felt like he was lying. He couldn't know that. But sometimes a bit of bravado was all a man had when he was about to charge into battle.

Claudia crossed the distance between them and raised herself up until her lips met his. There was an edge of desperation to the kiss, not exactly sexual, but full of every hope and dream that she might possibly possess.

And Drake could do nothing less than return the kiss with everything in his heart and soul.

It might have gone on for a second, or it might have gone on forever. Claudia was the one to pull back. "You better come back to me." It was a demand.

"You have my word."

And he hoped that the monster didn't make a liar out of him.

CHAPTER
FIFTEEN

WITH NO HUMANS TO CARRY, Sentinel and Drake made good time. A mix of Ruzo's intel and the information from the tracker they were following had them crossing the sky to the monster's lair in less than two hours. It might have taken days if they were marching through unfamiliar jungle. This was the monster's playground and he knew every passage and trail in the area. He could cross distances in times that seemed impossible to anyone else, but it had to do just with his knowledge of the area.

At least that was what Drake hoped. An invisible monster was one thing. An invisible monster with super-speed might truly be invincible.

Sentinel stayed in the air while Drake landed and shifted to his warrior form, claws at the ready and skin covered in a fine sheen of scales that would offer some protection. If something went wrong, Sentinel would be able to see it. At least that was the hope. And Drake might be able to get away.

The first evidence of life that Drake saw was a burnt out campfire. Not even a wisp of smoke emanated from it, but he could smell the memory of a fire in the air. In the distance, a collection of branches, vines, and leaves had been woven together to make something like a hut.

Was that where the monster slept?

Drake was braced for an attack at any moment. He was in the monster's territory. But nothing rushed at him. He was tempted to call out since he didn't see any of the people that he was looking for, but he was cautious enough to keep his silence.

Around the back of the hut, Drake found a stock-pile of old weapons and explosive charges, and a knee deep pile of broken communicators.

Beside that was a pile of bones. And based on the shapes and quantity, they weren't all from the same person.

He had to get their people out of there. And fast.

Drake kept searching, picking up the pace as much as he dared. The longer it took, the more he was worried that Ruzo's escape had spurred the monster into action. Would he just find a pile of bodies?

Then a faint noise caught his ear. Drake went

running, unsure if it was a trap or not. At this point, he needed to find *something*.

Who he found was Fluke.

As reported, the dragon was in bad shape. He was pale and sweating and his leg was twisted completely the wrong way. His hands were bound behind him with thick vines that must have been taken from the jungle. Given the state his body was in, no wonder he hadn't shifted into one of his other forms and taken off. It was a dangerous thing to do when the body was tied up. It took concentration. The kind of pain that he must be feeling from his broken leg was probably enough to make shifting impossible.

"Drake? Is that you?" The words were surprisingly clear given the groan of pain that had summoned Drake. "Is this a fucking joke? He got you too?"

Drake crouched by him and held up his unbound hands. "I'm not a prisoner. We came for you. Where is that thing? Where are the others?" Fluke was alone, though Drake could see where Ruzo must have been tied next to him. A pile of ash and burned vine showed what had bound him.

"Others? Did that mercenary not get away?" Fluke shifted where he sat and groaned in pain as he jolted his leg. He let out a stream of curses and settled back into his original position.

"We found him," Drake confirmed. He stayed far

enough back so that he wouldn't accidentally touch Fluke. He didn't want to make his injuries worse. "But it got the other two mercenaries and Vise. Have you seen them?"

Fluke cursed again. "No. Haven't seen anything since Ruzo got away."

"And the monster? Is he here?" Drake wished that he could trust his eyes, but that wasn't possible. Instinct told him the monster wasn't there. Otherwise he would've already been attacked.

"Not here," Fluke confirmed.

Then he had to take the opportunity that he had. "I'm coming back for you." Drake promised. "I just have to go signal to Sentinel. He's in the air."

Fluke nodded and flinched as he shifted minutely. "I'm not going anywhere."

Drake was concerned that was a final kind of truth and not a temporary one. They had a med kit with them, but they didn't have the means to fix Fluke's leg. Shifting might fix it for good, but they would need to take care of the pain for him to become able to concentrate enough.

Drake sent off the signal for Sentinel to land and was joined by the other dragon a few minutes later. He reported what he found and Sentinel went off to help Fluke, med kit clutched in his hands and a determined look on his face.

Sentinel was the one with medical training, so it was up to Drake to explore the rest of the camp and find the others.

He walked a wider circumference this time and he found who he was looking for after another half hour. Krax and Seris were both tied up and bickering with each other while Vise was in an unconscious pile next to them, her hands also tied behind her back. But the three of them looked relatively unharmed, except for Vise's unconsciousness. Thankfully, all of their bones seemed to be in working order.

If Vise could be roused and could fly, they could get out of here in no time. "I told you they were coming," said Krax in a triumphant tone. "You owe me fifty credits."

"That's the asshole who let me get snatched." Seris glared at Drake. "Take the credits from him."

He wasn't touching that comment, even as it was a reminder of his shame. "You guys ready to get out of here?" Drake asked. He would give them whatever credits they needed if that settled the score. He doubted Seris would accept an apology.

"More than ready," said Krax, straining uselessly against his bonds.

"Any idea where that monster is?" It was getting more and more concerning that the monster wasn't at his camp.

Neither Krax nor Seris had an idea. How often did it go to hunt? Drake wondered. And what was it hunting?

Dread pooled in his belly, and he really wanted to get out of the camp.

But maybe this was its own kind of opportunity. He remembered the explosive charges he'd seen behind the hut. A dangerous thing to keep lying around. And maybe exactly what they needed. They needed to get rid of the invisible monster, but that didn't mean they had to fight it head on.

He helped untie Seris, Krax, and Vise. And he was just about to go and find Sentinel to see if he had anything that would help wake the dragon up when Vise groaned and blinked her eyes open. She took a look around and let out a string of curses that might have made Drake blush in other circumstances.

"That thing got me, didn't it? It got you too?" She squeezed her eyes shut and groaned again.

Why did everyone keep thinking that? "I'm the rescue party." Drake grinned. "Come on. It's time to get out of here."

It took Vise a few minutes to struggle to her feet, but then he led them all towards Sentinel, who had managed to give Fluke enough drugs to have the man smiling and laughing. He'd done nothing for the leg. At this point, the only chance Fluke had of fixing it without a fully trained doctor and med suite was shifting to his dragon form. "That's everyone," said Sentinel. "Are we ready to go?"

"No." Drake shook his head. "I think we need to leave a little parting gift for our monstrous friend. How do you feel about explosives?"

CLAUDIA WAS okay for the first hour or so after Drake left. She tidied up the already near spotless galley and even indulged in a small snack from the food processor. The fruit practically melted on her tongue, and she didn't know if she could go back to eating those terrible nutrition bars after one taste of it.

But after she was done with her snack, she had to give up the galley and admit there was nothing else to do in there. She hadn't been forbidden from going to any part of the ship, so she spent a little time exploring, looking around the cockpit and glancing down the narrow hallway that would lead to the sleeping quarters. It wasn't a large ship, but it was very nice. Very expensive.

Mercenaries didn't fly in ships like this. Most of their vehicles were on the verge of falling apart and limping from one job to the next. That was, unless the mercenaries were working with one of the bigger outfits, in which case they were often better equipped than certain militaries.

Not that that was any use against a monster.

No. Claudia put thoughts of the monster aside. She wasn't going to think about it. Drake and Sentinel were going to deal with it, and they knew what they were doing. They had to.

That thought lasted just until she turned another corner and accidentally found the medical bay. Claudia looked through the door and froze.

Ruzo was laying on one of the beds with some kind of device clamped to his slowly rising and falling chest. The giant alien looked strangely small as he sat there, and Claudia couldn't figure out why she'd been scared of him before.

Funny how a couple dire days could change that.

She took a cautious step into the room and then another until she could sit on the stool beside his bed. She might not have known the man well, but no one deserved to be alone on their sickbed.

His cuts and bruises were healing rapidly as whatever the machine was doing took its effect. The kind of medical treatment available in space, even on a space ship millions of miles away from civilization, still astonished Claudia. What would they be able to do if they were on a planet and had access to a doctor?

Luckily, Ruzo seemed to be doing okay without a doctor. For now. But she didn't know enough about what the machine was or what it was doing to truly know his prognosis. Drake and Sentinel had been in too much of a hurry to go find the others that there hadn't been much time to explain Ruzo's prognosis.

What if something went wrong when she was alone with him? What if he died?

She vaguely remembered the CPR that she'd learned for a short lifeguarding gig more than a decade ago, but she wasn't sure that that was something that worked on aliens. Was Ruzo's heart where she would expect it to be? What about his lungs?

She curled her hands into fists to keep them from shaking and stared at Ruzo as if he could explain the inner workings of his anatomy, but the unconscious alien just lay there.

Claudia burst up from her seat and walked out of the med bay. She just needed a minute. She wouldn't leave Ruzo alone for long, not that he would care. Maybe she could go find a book or something to read to him. Or read to herself. She just needed to keep her mind off everything else.

Why had Sentinel said she was Drake's mate?

And there it was. The thing she was supposed to be ignoring. The thing she *had* to ignore to keep sane.

She couldn't think of this while Drake was off facing an invisible monster that had managed to snatch almost their entire team out from under them. What if he didn't come back? What if she never got the answers she needed?

What if he was her one chance at love and she'd already lost it?

Claudia groaned and leaned back against one of the metal walls as the questions assailed her. She started to slide down and knew she'd end up crumpled in the hallway if she let herself sink any further, so she pushed herself off the wall and kept moving.

She didn't mean to find the cargo ramp. Drake had taken the time to explain exactly how far the defenses of the ship reached, and the cargo ramp was well within them. She was technically safe here, but if the monster was lurking outside, it could see her.

And she couldn't see it. But she sucked in greedy gulps of the air around her, not even caring how humid it was. Being on a planet like this was grounding in a way that space never could be. And already her thoughts were starting to settle, just a little.

Drake would come back. They would have their talk. They would have *more* than their talk, as a matter of fact. They were going to see exactly where this thing between them wanted to go.

Claudia had made it out of impossible situations before. This was no different. It just sucked when she was the one waiting, instead of the one heading into danger.

Would this be her life if the bond between her and Drake went any deeper? Did he run off like this all the time? She didn't know if she could handle the emotional turmoil of that. And if he was running into danger, he better plan to take her with him.

These thoughts were leading nowhere. Claudia's mind drifted back to their rapid fight and fall as Vise was shot down right before they found Ruzo. She remembered manipulating fire, summoning it and shooting it out of her hands as if she'd been born to do it. Even now it was a little strange to consider.

Could she do it when she wasn't in danger?

Clearly it had something to do with the whole mate thing. It was a little hard to wrap her mind around, but at least it was something she could try.

Claudia held her hand out in front of her and stared at her palm. It didn't look any different. She imagined summoning a ball of fire as if she were some kind of superhero from a movie back home. She focused on it so hard that her temple began to throb and her eyes watered.

Her palm remained empty.

Okay, that didn't work.

She snapped her fingers and imagined she was lighting a match. While she made a resounding clicking sound, there was no fire to be found.

Did she need to be near Drake for it to work? Had he somehow summoned the flame for her when they were fighting the monster?

She wasn't going to give up so easily. She closed her eyes and took several deep breaths, pulling humid air deep into her lungs. She let her worries for Drake and Ruzo and Sentinel and the rest of them all melt away. Right now, this was just about the fire and finding it for herself.

She could feel the rumbling heat within her, something new deep in her gut that felt like it belonged, like it was filling some space that she hadn't realized was empty. She dug even deeper and imagined the heat from that space flowing out from within and manifesting in the air around her. Something tickled over her fingers and she opened her eyes.

Fire.

In her hand.

Claudia let out a whoop of joy, careful to keep her fingers still. She'd done it. It wasn't something she had just imagined.

Imitating what she'd done the first time she held

fire, she tossed it from hand to hand, playing with it as if it were some kind of flaming baseball. But after a few minutes, she let it go. She didn't want to accidentally damage the ship or set the ground around her on fire.

She was just about to head inside when a sound deep in the jungle caught her attention.

Was that Drake and the others returning?

Claudia strained to hear. It started as a low moan, something that barely registered over the rustling leaves around her. But eventually the word took shape.

"Help!"

A woman's voice. And full of so much pain. Could it be Vise? Had she somehow escaped the monster? The pleas for help grew louder.

Claudia looked back towards the ship and realized she'd already stepped down to the bottom of the ramp. It was still another meter or so until she would leave the boundary of the ship's defenses. Inside the boundary, she was safe. Anything outside was in danger.

She knew she shouldn't move another centimeter.

"Help! Please!" The cries were pure anguish.

Claudia couldn't leave Vise out there possibly bleeding out. The woman needed help. Besides, Drake and Sentinel were fighting the monster right now. It couldn't be in two places at once.

And she had fire. She wasn't defenseless.

That last thought was all she needed to take off running towards the sound of the voice.

She just made it past the ship's defenses when the air in front of her shimmered and glitched. She saw a tall figure with mottled green and gray skin. Only for a blink of an eye.

Something hit her and she crumpled to the ground, unconscious.

CHAPTER
SEVENTEEN

DRAKE WAS ready to get off this rock for good. The drugs that Sentinel had given to Fluke were enough to allow the man to shift into his dragon form and fly with them back to the ship. Vise was also alright to fly. And she and Sentinel were carrying Seris and Krax. Everyone was fine. Injuries, yes, but no deaths.

No need to delay any further. As soon as they were in the force field and secure, they were taking off.

Sentinel might have been the leader of this crew, but Drake didn't think that he would have any complaints about that.

And then he and Claudia could have their long-awaited talk.

Long-awaited? He'd known her for two days.

That was how mating worked, time didn't matter. She was his. Or she would be. As soon as they could get a moment alone together. But worry still had Drake all wrapped up. He hadn't wanted to leave Claudia alone. And the fact that they hadn't actually faced the monster was weighing heavy on him.

It felt like cheating to leave that camp wired to blow and just hope that the monster set off the charges.

What if some animal wandered across the territory and took the camp out instead?

Anyone who landed here would be prey for that thing. And from the piles of bones he'd found, it had happened plenty of times already.

Drake didn't know why the monster hadn't bothered to kill any of the crew yet. Maybe it liked to keep its meals alive for some time before feasting.

It didn't matter. They were all safe now. They could all go home.

They landed just outside the ship's defenses and Drake, Sentinel, and Vise all shifted back to their human forms while Fluke stayed in the air above them. Often times, shifting forms would heal broken bones, but it was no guarantee, and once he shifted back, his leg might be as mangled as it had been when they left.

"I'll go get the stretcher," Vise said and headed into the ship. Krax and Seris trotted after her.

Something still felt wrong. Maybe it was just that Claudia wasn't waiting for him with open arms. But he would see her in just a minute. As soon as he got on the ship.

A moment later, Vise came back with the stretcher and a dark look on her face. "Your human is gone," she said. "I scanned the ship for life forms and the mercenary in the med bay was the only man on board."

What? No. "That's wrong." The denial came straight out of Drake's soul. "She wouldn't just walk away."

"That's not what I said. But she's not here."

Drake met Sentinel's eyes and they shared a grim look. Claudia wouldn't leave the defenses unless she had a good reason. And the monster had been nowhere to be found.

"It has her," he said, absolute conviction in each of the words. "It's taking her back to its lair."

Sentinel didn't need to be told twice. He turned to Vise. "Get everyone settled," he commanded. "We're going back out there."

He and Drake launched themselves into the air and followed the same path they'd just taken towards the monster's lair. Drake flew as fast as he could, waiting to hear the blast go off in the distance and see smoke billow up into the air. The thought of it filled him with dread, and he pushed himself even faster, sprinting off in front of Sentinel and heedless of the fact that he was leaving his backup behind.

But he had to get Claudia. He called out for her with his mind, but either she didn't hear him or she was too far away to respond.

Maybe she was unconscious.

She couldn't be anything else. He refused to even consider the possibility.

They were coming up on the edge of the monster's lair, and from the air, Drake could see it was undisturbed. The charges hadn't been triggered. They still had time.

Then he heard the screaming.

Drake shot off towards it and sent a bolt of flame blindly down into the jungle. Claudia couldn't be hurt by it; as his mate she was immune to his flame. But the monster could. And he didn't need to see it to burn it.

He found his mate grappling with a being that was blinking in and out of sight. It was using some sort of invisibility shield, but it had clearly been damaged either from its earlier fight or from whatever Claudia was doing to it.

She was using his flame as if it had belonged to her for years.

She chucked balls of fire at the thing, and every

time they made contact, he got a better idea of what it looked like. Tall, skin that kind of looked camouflaged, long, *long* arms that were perfect for taking someone captive.

And teeth. It hadn't dug those teeth into anyone yet, but it was only a matter of time. And once it latched on, he was sure no one would escape its bite.

Sentinel finally showed up, and that was Drake's cue to dive into the fray. The monster had Claudia cornered and she was shuffling back, but she tripped over a fallen vine and went down hard.

That would've been it for her. He could see the anger in the monster's bearing. It wanted to finish her right there.

Drake sent a blast of fire at it and the monster scrambled back.

He didn't stop. Claudia was safe for now. The monster was distracted, and Drake sent the full force of his flame at the being who was trying to kill his mate. He unleashed enough fire to take out an entire battalion, and by the time he was done, the trees around it had already started to go up in flames and the monster had fallen, its shield finally giving out and its body lying there on the jungle floor, unmoving.

Dead.

Drake whipped around, ready to find Claudia and get her to safety.

But she was running straight towards the monster's lair and all of the explosives that were waiting to go off.

CHAPTER
EIGHTEEN

CLAUDIA TOOK off running the moment the fire rained down. It was pure animal instinct. She wasn't about to let herself get engulfed in flames.

Some part of her insisted that Drake would never put her in danger. Either he knew something she didn't or he didn't realize she was there. And if he didn't know she was there, she was still in trouble.

No time to dwell on it. There was an open path behind her and she took it.

She would have kept running forever, but a dragon swooped down in front of her. In between one blink and the next, Drake was there, shifting forms in less time than it took her to take a deep breath.

She barreled straight into him, and they crashed to the ground.

Drake's arms clamped around her and he held her

tight. "You're okay, it's okay. He's dead." The words washed over her and the heat of his body was a comforting inferno.

Adrenaline was making her shake. Her limbs felt funny, like she didn't quite have control of them. But she believed what Drake said and strangely—she couldn't understand why she did it or what it meant— she started laughing. She needed to do something, and that was her body's response.

Drake held on even tighter as the laughter quickly gave way to deep, heaving breaths that threatened to turn into sobs.

But she refused to cry. She had survived. She was alive. And he was right there with her.

"It mimicked Vise's voice," she said when she had a little bit of control back. "It sounded like she needed help. I couldn't just leave her out there." She needed Drake to know why. She hadn't taken a stupid risk. She'd done it to save someone.

He had to understand that. Instead of saying anything, he held her tighter.

A moment later, she heard footsteps and looked up to see Sentinel joining them.

"All good then?" he asked.

Drake didn't let her go when he answered. "All good. Though we should probably get rid of the trap."

"What trap?" Claudia asked. "Did you find the

others? What happened?" She'd been too focused on survival to worry about the others, but if Drake and Sentinel were here, then clearly something had happened.

Drake gave her a quick kiss as he stood and then pulled her to her own feet. "Sentinel and I need to take care of something really quick. We will tell you when we get back."

Claudia's mind was still reeling, and she didn't have time to demand more answers. Drake and Sentinel took off and returned several minutes later. She hadn't managed to do anything more than stand, her brain still catching up to the fact that the danger was over.

They were both grinning and Sentinel was carrying a large satchel full of something. He held it up. "No use letting ordinance go to waste," he said.

Ordinance? "Are you carrying a bag of explosives?" she asked. She took a cautious step further away from him.

"We rigged the monster's lair to blow," said Drake. "You were running right towards it."

Claudia didn't have a response to that. She'd been running straight towards a pile of explosives. If Drake hadn't stopped her, she would be scattered across a clearing in a million bloody pieces.

Nope. Her brain refused to process that. She had

dealt with the monster already. She'd figured out how to summon flame to her hands. That was enough. Any more and her brain might actually break in two.

"Are the others safe?" she asked again. "You clearly found the monster's lair."

Drake nodded and slung an arm around her. "They're all back at the ship. Let's go back and get off the stupid rock."

Claudia smiled. "Yes. Let's go."

It was an unexciting ride back. And once they were at the ship and away, things happened quickly. Sentinel and Drake got swallowed up in the action, and Claudia ended up finding quarters for herself. Once they were in the sky and safe to move around the ship, she found a shower and washed off the days of mud, grit, and jungle.

She was never going camping again. That simple.

But she wasn't exactly sure where she was going right now. Back to Drake's home planet apparently. But where was she going from there?

She scavenged some clothes from a communal drawer, and while they didn't fit perfectly, it was better than her dirty rags.

It was a while later that Drake knocked on her door. She let him in and smiled when she saw that they were wearing matching outfits and he looked just as clean and showered as she did.

Pity they hadn't showered together.

"There's some things we need to talk about," Drake started. Of course. This was what she'd been waiting for. She knew it was coming, but now it was here, she was a little scared to get started.

"Do you want to sit?" She patted the small bed beside her. There wasn't any other place to sit in the room.

Drake looked at it and then looked at her. "Are you sure?" And there were layers to that question, layers she wasn't going to look at too closely.

She patted the mattress.

Drake sat beside her. They were quiet for a moment and that was it.

They were alone. They were safe. And Claudia knew they could save the talking for later.

Drake opened his mouth, but whatever he was planning to say, she swallowed it up with a kiss, shifting herself until she was on his lap, legs strad-dling his and fingers woven through his hair. He groaned against her and she could feel his cock, the promise of the length of it pressed between them.

It was Claudia's turn to moan and arch against him as she leaned down and kissed his neck, his jaw, and then finally back up to his lips.

A growl caught in the back of Drake's throat, primal enough to make her shiver. He tugged her impossibly closer to him. She didn't think they could get even a centimeter closer. At least not until they took their clothes off.

Why were they still dressed?

She might have asked it, but she lost herself in the kiss once more. Thoughts of danger, of monsters, melted away. For now, she was finally safe, and she didn't need to care about anything except the feel of Drake in her arms.

Exactly where he was supposed to be.

With a bump of his hips and his hands cradling her body, he flipped them so he was on top of her, her back against the narrow bed. He loomed over her, his face half in shadow, almost unrecognizable. But already she knew his body, his scent, the feel of him against her.

Was this what he meant when he said mate?

She could have asked. He was looking at her so sincerely, lust and passion warring with some softer emotion.

But Claudia wasn't in the mood to talk, not while her body was on fire with need.

Before he could even try to talk, she reached a hand around his neck and pulled him closer, hungry for more of his kiss. He could use any word he wanted to describe this thing between them. It didn't matter. Whatever it was, it was real. And she just wanted him.

All of him. Every inch of his hard, delicious body pressed against hers as they danced this ancient dance together.

Drake's fingers teased the stretchy waistband of the pants she'd pilfered until he managed to tug them down a bit, exposing her hips to the cool air of the room. Their bodies could only do so much to warm it.

So they'd have to stay close. Not that she was complaining.

His fingers glided over the shirt she was wearing and for the craziest moment she thought he might tear it off of her with some sort of secret dragon strength.

Instead, he kept heading down until he could tug her pants off completely and expose her.

Fuck. Yes.

Her legs fell open, and she was gratified by the groan that Drake let out.

And then he was on her, his lips pressed against her tight sex, and pleasure zinged through her, lighting her up.

Claudia wanted more, needed it, spreading her legs wider as he licked her with the kind of passion only a dragon could give her. She shuddered, every nerve on fire as the pleasure washed over her. His tongue made her want to babble out wicked promises, but she wasn't sure she had a handle on her vocabulary right now, too caught up in what he was doing to her.

She never wanted him to stop.

Drake's growl was something that made her want even more, the sound vibrating against her as he licked her even faster, more desperately. She was helpless against it and her body gave up the fight, shuddering against him as she came with a cry.

The room around her went a little hazy as she tried to recover, but Drake gave her no quarter. Not that she really wanted him to.

She wanted everything from him, but not that. Not right now.

He pulled his shirt over his head and tossed it somewhere, and Claudia shivered again as she took in the swell of his muscles, the way it corded down him, pure power and purpose.

All hers.

Then his pants were gone and she forgot how to breathe.

Oh.

Wow.

His hand wrapped around his impressive cock, stroking once, then again, that sexy groan of his back in his throat. She couldn't resist the temptation and reached out, covering his hand with her own. Drake shuddered against her and his jaw clenched.

It was a beautiful thing to watch that much power contained in one man, to know he was exerting his massive control just for her.

But she didn't want control. Not from him. Not right now.

She needed anything but that.

And when he moved forward, brushing away her hand and guiding himself to her entrance, that was what she got. He pressed inside her, slowly at first, but she needed even more than that.

And he was ready to give.

Passion and lust wracked them both as they moved together, their bodies slick with sweat and caught in an elemental rhythm. Claudia wanted to hold onto it. She wanted to wrap this moment up in her memory and keep it there forever. It wouldn't be her last time with Drake, she didn't need any promises from him to know that.

But it was the first. And how could she forget that?

But they were both riding high on pleasure and need, and it didn't take much until they were both crying out, Drake's massive body covering hers as he thrust into her over and over again.

This was what she needed. This was what she wanted.

Just him and her. Here and together.

She didn't stand a chance at holding out, and

before long she cried out again as her body crested and Drake joined her with a shudder, emptying himself deep into her.

Claudia floated on the pleasure in an impossible kind of contentment.

"Holy shit." She wasn't sure her heart would ever stop racing and her body was so sated she might never get out of this bed.

Drake had a warm arm around her and made a contented noise in the back of his throat.

Yeah, she could get used to this.

She was too happy to be nervous and her words came easily. "So this whole mate thing? What's that about?"

"Sounds like you've already figured out a lot of it." He laid kisses along her neck. "You can summon my flame. You can talk to me telepathically. You're my mate. What more is there to know?"

Did it really need to be any more complicated than that? "It's just that simple?"

"Stay on Vemion with me and see."

For the last three years, Claudia had been journeying across the galaxy and exploring every corner and nook and cranny of space. She had never taken a moment to slow down and really enjoy a place. But not on purpose. Could she really find a home on a planet full of dragons?

"Are there invisible monsters that are going to hunt us through the jungle? Because that's a dealbreaker." She had had more than enough of that to last a lifetime.

A laugh burst out of Drake and he kissed her again before pulling back. "You're going to love it."

Yeah. It sounded really good.

ONE YEAR *later*

"I told you I wasn't getting out of this bed for a week, and I meant it." It was one hell of a bed. Claudia played with the sheets, wrapping her fingers around the fabric and tugging until it revealed her naked leg. She wiggled her toes at Drake, who was standing expectantly at the edge.

"You don't remember what today is?" he asked. He was wearing one of his formal suits, a green and black affair that she wanted to rip off of him in pieces until she could pull him back down to join her for a day spent under the covers.

Claudia remembered. And she groaned. "Your mother. No." Drake had told her plenty of stories about his mom in the last year.

The first one had been about the ultimatum she'd

set before disappearing for an entire year. It had been a bit of a shock. The same shock that came from finding out her mate wasn't just some normal dragon, but an actual lord with a title and property and everything. She didn't want to be a lady. But she was his, and it came with the territory. And the estate was a nice bonus.

"You go meet her." That sounded good. Claudia could just stay right where she was. And he could come back and join her whenever he was ready.

Drake came around the side of the bed and wrapped his fingers around hers. "Come on, love. We have to do this."

"I never signed up for this." It was one thing to face almost certain death by journeying through a wormhole. Meeting her boyfriend's mother? Yeah, way scarier. Especially since the woman was supposed to be some sort of high-level diplomat with exacting standards.

"Come on." Drake dragged her towards the edge of the bed, but it wasn't like she was resisting. And with a final complaint, Claudia climbed out and followed him towards the dressing room where her gown was waiting.

It was a gorgeous thing, something she definitely would have loved if she didn't have to wear it for the scariest meeting of her life.

"What do you think her decision will be?" she asked as she pulled on the outfit and started adjusting her hair. "Especially given the situation with your brothers."

There was no way his mother could've predicted what had happened over the last year. Claudia thought Cipher and Storm's mates were great. But they weren't exactly proper dragon ladies.

Drake wrapped his arms around her and gave her a thorough kiss. "I love my mother. I am going to be happy to see her. But I don't care what she says today. I have you. I would give up one hundred inheritances if that's what it took."

Claudia's smile threatened to break her face. "Let's not get ahead of ourselves there, buddy. Your house is pretty nice."

"Our house," he corrected.

Right. Because all that was his was hers. Still difficult to get her head around.

"You know I'd stick with you even without all this." She waved a hand around to emphasize what she was saying.

Drake kissed her again. "I know."

One kiss led to another. Claudia was tempted to drag him back to bed. It was right *there*. And far more pleasurable than anything else they had to do today.

But she forced herself to pull away. "Come on,

mate. We faced an invisible jungle monster. Your mom can't be any worse than that."

Drake tipped back his head and laughed. "I'm going to remind you that you said that."

And with an amused sort of dread, Claudia followed him out of the house. She wasn't sure what this meeting with his mother would hold, but it didn't matter. Because she had her mate and he had her. And if she'd ever doubted that her impossible mission through the wormhole was worth it, those doubts were long gone.

She was right where she belonged.

Thank you for reading Drake!

Here's what you should read next:
Check out a new alien world in Synnr's Saint, the first book in the Zulir Warrior Mates series.

Taken from Earth and used like a lab rat…
Emily was a normal law student until she was abducted by aliens. Forced to perform death defying feats by night and undergoing medical tests by day, she doesn't know how much longer she can take it. When one alien takes particular interest in her she's afraid things have gone from bad to worse. He's got

wings and fangs, and he makes her heart pound. But she can't want an alien like that... can she?

Read now!

KEEP IN TOUCH!

You can get a free full length sci-fi romance novel by joining my newsletter. You'll also be the first to know about great deals and new releases.
Sign up now!

Ready to give audio a try? Get a free audiobook here!

WHAT TO READ NEXT: SYNNR'S SAINT

Taken from Earth and used like a lab rat…

Emily was a normal law student until she was abducted by aliens. Forced to perform death defying feats by night and undergoing medical tests by day, she doesn't know how much longer she can take it. When one alien takes particular interest in her she's afraid things have gone from bad to worse. He's got wings and fangs, and he makes her heart pound. But she can't want an alien like that… can she?

He doesn't have time to rescue a human…

Oz is on Kilrym for a reason, and it's not to rescue the ethereal performer who captivates him by night. But covert ops are impossible when his mind is on the human who could be his fated mate. War is on the horizon, but what if the only way to save his people is to sacrifice Emily?

Despite the fact that they were born light years apart, they are a perfect match. But Oz is keeping secrets, and when Emily finds out the truth she may never be able to forgive him, no matter how much she needs him to survive and escape the planet alive.

Check it out!

INTERGALACTIC DATING AGENCY

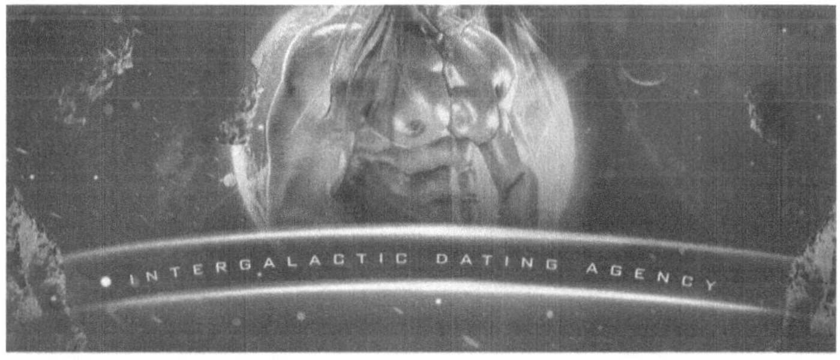

LOOKING for love that's out of this world? These strong, smart, sexy aliens are seeking mates from the Milky Way. Just hop onboard with your local Intergalactic Dating Agency. Join our group of authors as we explore the friendly skies and beyond with trilogies of cosmic craving, astral adventure, and otherworldly lovers. Warning: abductions may or may not be included!

ALSO BY KATE RUDOLPH

Looking for something else? Kate Rudolph has a heart pounding collection or paranormal and sci-fi romance stories for you! Bundles, bears, audiobooks, aliens, and more. Check out your options in the list below. You can find out all you need to know at www.katerudolph.net.

Want to check out one of the books? Click on the series name to find out more!

Dragon Brides

Fated mates, fierce women, and dragon princes.

Also available in audio!

Crux

Ranger

Saber

Cipher

Storm

Drake

Alien Mates: Planet Exile

Guerran is no place for pretty human women. But these alien heroes will protect their mates!

Also available in audio!

Exile's Hunter

Exile's Adored

———

Zulir Warrior Mates

Kidnapped humans. Alien Warriors. Electric wings.

The Zulir Warrior Mates series brings you human heroines and heroes abducted from Earth who find love – and wings! – with the alien warriors who rescue them.

Also available in audio!

Synnr's Saint

Synnr's Hope

Synnr's Spark

Synnr's Kiss

———

Guarded by the Shifter

Werewolf. Bodyguard. Mate.

The origins of these shifters are shrouded in mystery, but they're determined to protect their mates from any harm that comes their way.

Also available in audio!

Hunting Season

On the Prowl

Stalking Magic

Hungry for the Wolf

Detyen Warriors

Detya was destroyed a hundred years ago. These doomed warriors are out to find justice… and their mates.

The Detyen Warriors series brings you kick butt heroines, alpha alien heroes, fated mates, and relationships strong enough to span the galaxy!

The entire series is also available in audio!

Soulless

Ruthless

Heartless

Faultless

Endless

Alien Holiday Romance

Christmas… in space????

These alien holiday romances look beyond Earth's winter holidays and ring in the season across the galaxy! ***Select titles available in audio.***

Snowed in with the Alien Beast

The Alien's Winter Gift

The Alien Reindeer's Wild Ride

Trapped with her Alien Mate

Alien Outlaws

Outlaws, schemes, and love… it's all there in the Alien Outlaws series…

Andie Munster is sick of life on Ixilta, the planet she got dumped on after being abducted from Earth six years ago. And when the mysterious and dangerous Xandr shows up looking for a way off the planet, she's half-prisoner, half-co-conspirator in a wild rush to escape.

Rogue Alien's Escape

Rogue Alien's Woman

Rogue Alien's Secret

Rogue Alien's Legacy

Mated to the Alien

Fated Mate Alien Romance

Detyens are doomed to die young if they don't find their fated mates.

Follow along as these mated pairs fight off aliens, corrupt dictators, prejudiced humans, pirates, and more! The books can be read or listened to in any order, though some characters show up in multiple stories.

Select books available in audio.

Pick a book and jump into the action today!

Ruwen

Tyral

Stoan

Cyborg

Krayter

Kayleb

Shayn

Braxtyn

Doryan

Dekon

———

Stealing the Alpha

The thief takes what she wants, but the alpha keeps what's his...

Join shifter thief Mel as she clashes with lion alpha Luke in an explosive trilogy of two opposites who can't keep away from one another.

Also available in audio!

The Alpha Heist

Entangled with the Thief

In the Alpha's Bed

———

Save with box sets!

Aliens. Shifters. Warriors. Mates. Get them all wrapped together in these special box sets. Save up to 30% off the price of buying the individual books, depending on the series!

Alien Outlaws: The Complete Series

Mated to the Alien Volume One (also available in audio)

Mated to the Alien Volume Two (also available in audio)

Mated to the Alien Volume Three

Mated to the Alien Volume Four

Stealing the Alpha: The Complete Series (also available in audio)

The Mate Bundle

Detyen Warriors Volume One (also available in audio)

Detyen Warriors Volume Two (also available in audio)

Zulir Warrior Mates Volume One (also available in audio)

Standalone Paranormal and Sci-Fi Romance:

Crashed

Mated on the Moon

Mated to the Alien Dragon

Marked

Bear in Mind

Alpha's Mercy

Gemma's Mate

Find more by Kate Rudolph at www.katerudolph.net

ABOUT KATE RUDOLPH

KATE RUDOLPH IS paranormal and sci-fi romance writer who lives in Indiana. She loves writing about kick butt heroines and the steamy heroes who love them. She's been devouring romance novels since she was too young to be reading them and had to hide her books so no one would take them away. She couldn't imagine a better job in this world than writing romances and sharing them with her fellow readers.

If you enjoyed this story, please consider leaving a review.

www.ingramcontent.com/pod-product-compliance
Lightning Source LLC
Chambersburg PA
CBHW030641190726
48286CB00008B/2603

9 781953 748430